THE STORM

T.L. FUNK

Primix Publishing
11620 Wilshire Blvd
Suite 900, West Wilshire Center, Los Angeles, CA, 90025
www.primixpublishing.com
Phone: 1-800-538-5788

Published by Primix Publishing: 03/08/2024

ISBN: 979-8-89194-076-5(sc)
ISBN: 979-8-89194-077-2(e)

Library of Congress Control Number: 2024902935

CONTENTS

'The raindrops pound the ground hard matching the sound of her heartbeat, and her heavy breathing as she runs through the darken woods for her life she didn't know where he was or, but she had to escape. She has never been more frighten in her life than at that moment, again the rug has been pulled out from under her, first her father and now Jared, who she thought loved. Sabrina felt her feet hit something she didn't know what, but the sharp pain landing hard on the ground with her right knee causing her to scream out, then she heard Jared's voice screaming for her that she was a died woman when he finds her. She felt herself breathing hard and the pounding rain kept on coming, adding to the pain of her body than a loud clapped of thunder could be heard from the storm ahead.

" S-A-B-R-I-I-N-A, where are you bitch, you can run all you want I will find you no matter where you go! Sabrina where are you, come out, come out wherever you." Jared's voice sounded calmer and close somewhere in the darkness, coming from the direction of the cabin where Sabrina's worse fears came true from the man, she thought loved her, now wants to kill her.

The soft voice in her head told her to get up, while her small body wanted to remain lying on the muddy ground, she wanted to drown in the mud and water that surrounded her, her heart and body were in so much pain she wanted to just give up.

Jared continued to shout her name and she laid there still when she saw him from a far hoping and praying, he didn't see her.

Sabrina waited for Jared to leave in the direction of the cabin he was holding the left side of his face where Sabrina stabbed him.

Sabrina got up fast as if she was in a bad dream running being chased by him, leaving her old life for good. "SABRINA!!!" Jared shouts out. Sabrina shot up laying on her bed from another clap of thunder from the storm that was coming, breathing hard.

◆◆◆◆◆

CHAPTER 1

The Storm

The blazing hot sun heating the already baked ground of Texas as a dark, watery figure comes into view the soft roaring sound of a Arch motor fills the vast empty space as Jack speeds down the long, lonely road heading home, the static voice of the morning deejay filled the airwaves through Jack's radio saying "It's going to be hot, folks, 98 degrees and still climbing with no rain in sight, with a slight breeze, it's not even noon yet!" 'Trapper' Williams the deejay shouted across the air to anyone who would be listening. "No-o kidding!" Jack glared at his radio as he felt the sweat dripping down his skin, soaking his white tee and his thick black leather jacket didn't help ease his suffering.

Jack takes his red bandanna from his back pocket of his blue jeans to whip the sweat from the back of his neck. He looks up at the cloudless sky silently cursing the man upstairs for making his return home hell, but no matter the cost to him. Jack had to return to amend what he had caused his family especially with his old man who received the full force of his fist, the night after his graduation when things finally came to blows.

Jack races down this lonely road heading towards his small beachside town. he recalls the past few years with all that he has accomplished with his music now he wants to share the wealth with his folks, he is afraid of his parent's reactions from the way he left the last time he saw them which kept him from returning home, until now.

Jack stormed out of Midnight, Texas with his old man, Alan sitting on the kitchen floor with his mother, Julia kneeling at his dad's side, with her tears filling her green eyes pleading with him to stop this fight before it got worse as he watched his old man touching the corner of his lower lip, where blood began to form, after Jack pouched and shoved him to the ground from their biggest fight ever in their once close father and son bond Jack felt it coming for a long time they were both stubborn and hot heads from his dad's native American blood racing through his veins and his mother's Irish and German temper didn't help them.

Alan quickly got to his feet, grunting in pain trying to get up, to face his son glaring and shouting at him "Get the HELL out of his house and don't you ever come back, you hear me!!!" with a hard shove back and pointing toward the front door with tears filling his dark eyes.

Jack couldn't bear the hurt look on his dad's face, over his stupid future, how this war started he didn't know. Jack wanted music and his father wanted college so he could take over the Diner.

Jack quickly grabbed what he could, and shoved into his duffel bag, ran out into the storm that was a broaching that night as he raced toward his dirt bike that he and his dad built together before he started high school. Jack hopped onto his bike he gave his childhood home before roaring his bike to life one last look at his childhood home with his parents standing at the doorway with a hurt on their faces as he left haunted him in his dreams at night. Jack sped away without looking back, out of everything he has done in his life good or bad that was one of his greatest regrets he needed to fix before time runs out for him and his dad.

CHAPTER 2

There is no cure for these summer blues!!!

The steam billowed out from the crock pot, washing over her sweat bathed face, Sabrina wiped the sweat from her brow with the back of her hand, as she pours the Chicken noodle soup into the soup bowl preparing a lunch order for one her hungry customer. She looks through the serving window toward the crowded lobby of Big Al's diner. It felt much busier this time around, with the locals and the tourists spending their summer vacations here who could blame them with the white sandy beaches that line the coast which causes anything around her to feel stuffy, but she didn't mind it the diner kept her busy which was good for her felt normal for once.

Sabrina wished she was out there laying out or taking a walk enjoying the cool breeze and then burying her feet in the wet sand, hold hands with a beautiful man. That was her fantasy two years ago when she ran away from home New Kirk, Idaho and making her way towards Midnight, Texas to have a fresh start and to hide her from her past that is still out there looking for her.

Sabrina is frightened to death that her ex-boyfriend would find her here to destroy the life that she has worked so hard to build and hurt the people that she has come to care for like a family something she never had before in her life, Julia, Tony, and Alan.

She even found her long-lost father, whom she had not seen in 22 years, who runs a well-known hotel chain here called the Charleston.

Sabrina slowly scans the lobby looking for that familiar face of her past or maybe someone new that might come through that glass door maybe that handsome stranger from her fantasy. Then she lets out a sigh, of self-doubt and frustration, wondering if that stranger will ever show up, to show her that real love exists, but self-doubt always wins out in the end for her she hasn't met anyone that she found worthy enough to grab her attention.

Oh, she has received attention from men, so far, the verbal, physical and almost sexual abuse from those whom she thought should have treated her like she was a princess like her stepfather and her biological father who abandoned her when she was a young girl. She remembers that moment as if it was yesterday her father would tell her that he loved her with all his heart then turn away from her and walking towards the front door without her, taking a way her save, happy life and the belief that love was real, Sabrina sadly looked at her reflection in the silver metal toaster, her long blonde hair wet with sweat, with wisps of straight blonde coming lose from her rubber band from her ponytail and her make-up almost gone she looked, like she was a drowned rat and then a run way model, 'oh, please like she thought she was pretty enough to be a model, she shoved the toaster away not wanting look at herself anymore.

Sabrina has been told that she was pretty by those she has served and worked with, but never was told she was beautiful by anyone that she desired or cared about including Jared her ex and not even her father, though he has told her she was pretty, she only thought he was saying that to make himself feel better for abandoning her all those years ago to be raised by her abusive step-father and mother who lived and worked on the streets for drugs and sex.

Sabrina could not count how many times she was told how ugly and worthless she was by her stepfather until he saw how much money he could make off her teenage body when he noticed one his wife's high paying johns eyeing and drooling over Sabrina when she was 15 years old.

The large sum of money this 'John' was willing to pay to be her first time. A shiver rushed through her as she recalled the horrible beating she received when she took that cash cow anyway when she snuck out to sleep with the quarterback of her high school football team.

She remembers crying so much for her long-lost father to come and save her like he promised he would but didn't. She doesn't know if she will ever truly forgive him for walking away from her all those years ago.

Somehow Sabrina found the courage to walk away from that hell hole or so she thought until she met and fell in love with Jared the most beautiful man, she ever laid her eyes on.

Jared was five years older than her 19 years, but he was tall, medium built beautifully to her, with his sandy blonde hair and icy blue eyes that some said they could see the devil in those eyes, to Sabrina, she didn't care what they said about him, she was head over heels in love with him. Jared showered her with things that she never had before like flowers, gifts and a beautiful apartment that looked over the town and something that she longed for, but never received in her life love or what she thought was love, until she found out the real reason he hooked with her, was to use her connections to the bank that she worked for, the full access she had to the personal information and accounts that the bank had on almost everyone that lived and worked in New Kirk.

Jared would secretly get this info when he came to visit her at her job. Jared would use that information to scam the people that he wanted to use for his personal and financial gains.

Sabrina didn't know when she came across several floppy discs and journals of what his plans when she found the stash hidden in a briefcase in their shared walk-in closet when she decided to clean it out one day.

She found bank statements, that had her name and number from her personal computer at work and there was a cassette tape with Jared's voice confessing to another man whom she didn't recognize telling this mystery man what he was going to do and when he had all the money that he needed from all the accounts that he took from her computer that he would frame her for it and leave town, but Sabrina spoiled his plans when she went to confront Jared with what she had found, up at the cabin that they shared to together.

The man she thought she knew and loved turned into the devil that everyone warned her about when she threatens to expose him to the police and the people who trusted him with their money, but of course he strongly denied that he had anything to with the embezzlement, the scamming and that he was setting her up to take the fall for the crimes that he was committing on the people of New Kirk, but he didn't count on her showing him the evidence that she had on found him, he quickly turned on her, without thinking of an escape plan.

Jared quickly lunged at her, grabbing her by the shoulders and throwing her to the floor on the dining room table laid a 6th inch steak knife he grabbed, threatened to stab her with it as he slowly approached her with a calm, wick look on his face as she desperately crawled, to get away from him and looking for anything to use as a weapon against him she knew she couldn't overpower him with her petite size alone.

Sabrina quickly got up crying trying to make sense of what was happening to her with the man whom treated her like she was an angel was now trying to make her into an actual angel by threatening to kill her that he never loved her that he was just using her "where are you going Bitch there is no one here to save your sorry ass!" he mocked her in a sick and twisted toned voice like he wasn't the man she thought she loved, but someone she was trying to flee from!

Sabrina spies the poker by the fireplace she quickly grabs it starts swinging it, like a crazy woman causing him to back up, this was her only weapon of choice, she turns to face him eye to eye with the poker in hand and asking him "why did he do this, did he ever loved her or was the years they shared all a lie?!"

Jared looked at her and laughed, showing her his true colors to her that awful night, saying "how ugly and stupid," he thought, she was making her feel that she scum under his shoes, that he would pretend that she was a playboy model so he could stomach having sex with her the only thing he was interested in was the money that he would have made after he was done using everyone there in New Kirk and frame her for the crimes that he was committing on the innocent people of New Kirk with her connections to the bank that she works for, she wanted to cry has she felt her heart break into a million pieces, but she refused to let him see the hurt, her innocence was destroyed in that moment or what she thought was her innocence.

Then he lunged at her with the knife still in hand

causing her to jump quickly and with the poker still in hand swang at him like a crazy woman hitting him hard in the shoulder causing him to drop the knife, but then he lunged and grabbed her around the waist knocking them both to the floor!

Julia walks up beside Sabrina startling her out of her thoughts bring her back to the present asking her "Where is that blasted woman, Brenda, she is late again?!!" Julia fumed over their coworker's being late which shouldn't surprise them because Brenda was always late unless there was an important agenda for Brenda to be at work on time then she will be here, either it is about a man or money and sometimes it is both.

"Damn that woman!" Julia fumed loudly slamming the knife down hard on the counter causing Sabrina to jump a little startling her, Sabrina turned her head to look at the older, tiny Irish woman who took Sabrina in when she first came to Midnight, she had come to care deeply for this woman standing beside her as a mother figure sadly wishing her own mother was like Julia maybe her life won't have been such a mess.

Julia kind of remind Sabrina of Lucy in 'I love Lucy!" with her red curly hair and red paint lips, but she isn't into causing trouble like Lucy was, but she did have a sense of humor most of the time when Julia isn't bitching about the diner, Al, her husband, and this case Brenda being late again.

Brenda and Sabrina have never gotten along ever since Sabrina started working at Big Al's diner because Brenda life is all about drama, she has always been jealous of Sabrina's special bond with Julia. Brenda has always treated Sabrina like she was dirt under her feet and has tried several times to get Sabrina fired. Thank God, for Julia was Sabrina constant support and seeing through Brenda lies and schemes. If only Sabrina could stir clear from Brenda she would, but seeing Julia angry with Brenda, right now makes Sabrina want to beat the shit out of the bitch.

Sabrina decided to keep her thoughts to herself and turned towards the sink to work on the vegetables to rinse them and to keep her temper in check too.

Julia doesn't have red hair for nothing when Sabrina adds her two cents into the conversion trying to make light of the situation, she too gets annoyed with Brenda being late "OH you know Brenda! She was probably partying with her new older sugar daddy that she met here last night. Don't you worry thou; she will be here!" she said confidently knowing Brenda better than anyone she can read Brenda like some trash mag or novel.

Julia turns towards Sabrina to look at her with a smirk on her face "And how do you know this?" Julia asks, giving Sabrina a questioning look on her face, raising her left eyebrow at her along with the smirk. "You're not a psychic, are you?" "No!" Sabrina sang while shaking her head carrying the vegetables toward the table getting them ready to be chopped for the beef broth for the vegetable soup.

"Oh please, Brenda would not miss the chance to meet some of the sugar daddies that come in here for anything in the world, you know that silly."

Just then the doorbell jingled telling the waitresses that someone has entered the diner causing them to stop, to see who has come through the glass door just now. When they saw who it was walking through the lobby, Mr. Martin hobbled his way through with his cane in hand walking towards the front counter where Sabrina's station was for the day.

Sabrina and Julia looked at each other and giggled remembering what they had just talked about earlier. Mr. Martin was short, round, and balding with gray hair framed around his ears. Mr. Martin was kind of a grandpa type if Sabrina knew what a grandpa was, she never met hers, but she saw grandpas on TV shows Mr. Martin reminded her of them and a teddy bear when he was in a good mood which wasn't often.

Sabrina comes from the kitchen area, walks toward the front counter where Mr. Martin sat, she could tell that he was in his typical grumpy moods as his grumbles softly to himself, this lunch hour she approaches the counter, slowly to see if she could get him in a better mood "Hello, Mr. Martin, " Sabrina said cheerfully. "How are you this fine day?" Sabrina asks, taking her menu pad out of her apron getting ready to take his order "It would be a fine day if it weren't for this dam, heat!" Mr. Martin swore has Sabrina took the pen from her ear "I know what you're talking about." Sabrina answered agreeing with Mr. Martin about the hot temperatures outside as well as it was inside, especially with the air conditioner not working today. "Is there anything I can get for you today?" She patiently asked Mr. Martin answered back in a calmer voice "Yes, I will have a tall glass of lemonade and a…"

Moments later Brenda decides to make her grand entrance to get her dreadful day started, working at this tacky diner "Hello, everyone I am here!" Brenda proudly announced as she sashays her way toward the kitchen door makes her way through the sea of people that were watching her as if she was the queen of England, she looks at them as if they were peasants.

Brenda walks through the lobby making her way back toward the office to put her things away in her locker, but making sure all eyes are on her especially the men "And why not, after all, they are looking at perfection!" Brenda purred quietly to herself with her bleach, blonde hair perfectly was done up in a French twist, her make-up, and nails done to perfection, the years, the money that her sugar daddies and her boy toys lavished on her to get her body in a beautiful shape.

Brenda's boobs are big and perky, demanding attention with her round tight ass tightly wrapped into her pale pink waitress uniform and her long-tanned legs to match "How can any man resist me!" Brenda purred softly to herself and loving the power that she had over people especially men.

Julia was fuming, stared coldly at Brenda, a look of death would have killed Brenda instantly if she could. "Well-well, look who has decided to grace us with her presences, her Royal Highness, You're late!" Julia mocked, trying hard not to reach over towards Brenda to strangle the life out of her as they stood in the kitchen looking at each other. "Oh, well my clock didn't go off this morning, it's broken." Brenda cheerfully said as she shrugged her shoulders and waving her hand at Julia like it was no big deal to her if she was late, it annoyed the hell out of Julia, "Gees, Brenda, that's funny I thought you said you had that thing fixed last week!" Julia said trying to control her Irish temper.

"It is!" Brenda whined, pouting, trying to act all innocent, with Julia breathing down her neck. Brenda is going to have to do some major ass kissing for the next two weeks so she won't lose her job until her lands herself another sugar daddy.

"Oh, brother, here we go again!" Sabrina thought to herself as she rolls her eyes, shaking her head towards the two women as they began their daily bickering back and forth. Sabrina heads towards the kitchen to start Mr. Martin order.

"Holding out for a Hero-O-O-O!"

"Wel-ll, folks that was 'Holding out for a hero' by Bonnie Tyler," this is Trapper' Williams trapping you inside the radio hope to cool you down while you listen to your faves, from Country, to rock, to newbies and the oldies!" the DJ shouting across the airwaves "It's 99 degrees and rising. It's just past 2:00 o'clock!"

Jack takes his bandanna from his back pocket to whip the sweat from off his neck when he rounds the bend, he sees a sign off toward his right in the distance, as he gets closer to the sign Jack's heart begins to beat faster out of excitement or fear he reads "Welcome to

Midnight, Texas population 2000." As he entered his hometown it felt busier than he remembered.

Jack passes under a street banner that reads 'Welcome all to the Summer Festival'.

"Aaah, The Summer Festival, this is why the streets were so busy," Jack whispered to himself with a smile, as he thinks back on his boyhood days, how he had spent his whole allowance on the fairs and the carnivals to celebrate the beginning of summer and the end of school.

Jack smiles to himself as he recalls the wonderful memories of a boy long since gone.

The smells of popcorn, the grilled onions, and the barbecues were making him hungry by the minute, the trouble that he got himself into at the county fair, he almost got himself kicked out when he and his friends would sneak into the horse barn, setting off some fireworks. Jack smiles to himself "Aaah the good old days!" while shaking his head as he remembers when he looks at his reflection in his side mirror gone is the awkward teenage boy in place is this older black haired, wearing 'Top gun' aviator dark shades, rock and roll God to millions of his fans.

Jack passes the old Eastman Theater that housed the only movie screen in town. He remembers how he could not wait for that day when he got his allowance on Fridays after doing his chores.

He would buy the biggest soda pop and popcorn he could afford and sit in the back row and with his eyes glued to the big screen like it was a god.

Jack would be so focused on what was happening on that big screen that he would almost forget to breath when he watched Gene Autry and Roy Rogers galloping on their faithful steeds riding in saving the day, but his heart would race with excitement when he saw 'the King' sing, dance and slide down that pole in 'Jailhouse Rock'.

Jack lost count on how many times he had watched that movie. It was then that Jack knew what he wanted to do with the rest of his life.

"I am so glad to see that the people of Midnight have taken pride in that 100-year-old theater." Jack thought to himself as he continues to ride through this small beachside town as he passes the St. Joseph Cathedral church that was built during the Spanish wars, with its large gray stone walls, stain glass windows, and sky tall steeples beckoning believers and non-believers to come worship.

Jack has always believed in a higher power, but he feels the way a person looked and how they lived compared to the rest of the world is that person's business. To some, he looked a sinner because he lived his life like that of a Rockstar except for the drugs he worked to damn hard for that shit.

Jack continue to ride through the town passing the boardwalk piers that lined the coast, enjoying the feel of the sea breeze softly, caressing his skin like it was a lover's touch that kissed him that drifted slowly back and forth from the coast welcoming him back as he rides on the road that leads out towards his father's diner giving him time to think and the chance to back out since his parents aren't really excepting him home right now.

This would be the first time in a long time that he saw his folks because the last time was with his father on the floor and his mom kneeling beside him, with tears in her eyes on their living room floor after Jack punched his old man on the chin causing his father to fall on the floor with his father shouting him at to get out of his house to never to return.

Jack has never set foot in their house again until, now to right that wrong that he had caused, especially with his old man, with all his success in the music business would mean a damn thing to him if he can't share it with them, after all, it was his dad who got him, his first guitar he wanted to show him what he achieved with that guitar, because of their unconditional for him, He hoped.

Off in the distances, he sees his father's white brick diner he stops his bike to stare at it like it was a ghost from his past that has come to scare him away or lay to rest the ghost that has haunted him for years with his folks especially his old man.

CHAPTER 4

After Mr. Martin left the diner Sabrina was alone and for a brief moment, it was quiet, until she hears the door chimes ring again announcing that a customer had just entered into the diner. Sabrina looks up to see who the customer is, then she cringes when she sees whom the customer is Steve Hicks and his two minions Mr. tall and skinny and Mr. Chubby and short. Steven Hicks is this all-American boy that never had to work a day in his life because Mommy and Daddy took care of all his needs and wants.

Steven acted like he owned the whole world and everyone in it. He had been a thorn in Sabrina's side since she had started working at Big Al's Diner, but most of the time it has been verbal assaults and the slimy attention he would aim in her direction, but never done anything to warn her that he was dangerous, until now she got this strange vibe that something wasn't right because he had a sick, evil gleam in his icy blue eyes as he zeroed in on her again.

He rounded the large "L" shaped formic yellow stone stamped counter along with his tall friend both facing her with a hungry look on their faces and it wasn't for food either. His short and fat friend on the other side of the counter they all cornered her as if she was prey for their sick pleasure.

Sabrina felt her skin began to tingle that she sensed that she was in serious trouble, she didn't know how she was going to survive with what they might do to her, so she thought she would give them, her tough girl act to see if she could detour them from doing want with her, she was praying for a miracle. "Hey, this is the serving area, paying customers on the other side of the counter." Sabrina glared and snapped at Steven and his friends, pointing toward the other side of the counter.

Steve looks at his friends, with a sick chuckle in his voice and got in her face "I don't give a fuck!" he grabs Sabrina roughly by her small shoulders as if she was nothing him, he lefts her up quickly slamming her hard on top of the counter hurting her ass.

Sabrina felt Mr. Chubby's meaty hands on her shoulders holding her still on the counter so she couldn't struggle her way out with whatever they had in mind for her, she felt the sheer terror rush through her, she would have to fight like hell, if she had to die this night, then she will or do something to stop the rape about to happen she was praying with all of her might for a miracle, she looked up to the ceiling.

She knew that it would be for their benefit and not hers. "We have decided that you're going to be on the menu, and you are going to serves us all, right!" He said with an evil smile on his face he grabbed her by the throat with his right hand almost cutting off her air "Now open your fucking legs. I am coming in!" He demanded of her, she fought with all her might to get the chubby guy to let her go, but she felt herself losing this battle, so she leaned back to claw, spitting into his face and shouted with a strong NO! this was not her choice."

Steve touched the right side of his face, where her spit hit his cheek. He glares at her with a cold look in his eyes. Steven wears back as if he was going to give her a hard backhand or something.

Sabrina quickly closed her eyes readying herself for the hard blow that never came, she heard a loud thud and Steve groaned in pain, cursing up the storm after the countertop jump.

CHAPTER 5

Jack rides slowly towards the entrance to the parking lot where the tiny white brick Diner, except for the two large storm windows and a glass door in the center that faced the road, that serve the best half-pound hamburger and fries in town that cause Jack's mouth to water just thinking of them, the old place hasn't change since the day his father open the doors when he was 12 years old, Jack sits just staring at the old place, with Jack's heart began to beat faster with what might await him beyond that glass door when he opens it "Will they welcome me home with open arms or will they give me the cold shoulder and banded me for life?" Jack thought to himself, hoping for the latter. Jack rolls forwards into the parking lot.

Jack stops before getting closer to the Diner he has

never been so nervous in his life, not even standing in front of a stadium full of his screaming fans made him this anxious.

Jack scans the area that surrounds him and the Diner before him, there are the corn and wheat fields on the other side of the road Jack remembers how his father had to beg the farmer that owned the land, that his dad bought the acre of land where the Diner sits now so he could build it to support his family too, he also promised a free meal, to seal the deal Jack continue his look around him, in the distances he can see the mountain peeks of Lookout Mountains where he would go camping to clear his head and write the songs for his music.

There is a very special place up there that he discovered when he was 16 when he first got his bike that place was magical it was quiet and beautiful where he found himself.

Jack slowly rolls further into the parking lot of his dad's Diner taking the first spot near the glass door spies a red sports car parked in the spot on the other side of the glass door.

He looked at his reflection in the side mirror, fixing his hair a little trying to calm his nerves climbing off his bike, began walking towards the glass door stops taking a deep breath saying to himself. "Well, it's now or never!" as the king would say.

Jack pushes open the door to go inside, then scans the room and smiles to himself like time hasn't even touched the place, since the last time he was here, he recalls. The night he graduated, his folks threw him the biggest graduation party ever and the last time they were a happy family.

Jack looks around him the lobby had the same old 50's look with two large over stuff cherry red leather booths that curved at the ends on each side of him as you entered the diner, they lined the large bay windows that seated 4 or more people that had a large rectangle dark brown stained hardwood table.

Past them are 4 smaller squared tables that had the same dark brown stained, hardwood with the same dark stained wood winged back chairs, past those are two large round with the same dark stain table and chairs that could sit a larger group of people, beyond the tables was the large L shaped yellow stone stamped formic, counter that had 8 bright red cherry leather bar stools that lined the counter are bolted to the black and white checked floor.

Then a very loud lady shouted "No!" snapped him out of his looking over the place he looked around him to see where the scream came from, what he saw chilled him to the bone was a beautiful woman sitting on the counter being pinned with three guys surrounding her and a look of shear panic was set in her eyes. Jack rushes to the young woman's defense assuming she was a waitress with the uniform she was wearing. Jack grabbed the sandy hair guy Jack thought was the gang leader by the arm and body slammed the mother fucker hard on top of the counter shocking everyone except for Sabrina she still had her eyes closed readying herself for the hard blow against her check from Steve which never came, instead a sound of a hard thud and Steve groaning and cursing at someone as gusted of air touched her check.

She then heard someone else's voice that caused Sabrina to opened her eyes suddenly she was speechless, what stood in front of her was the most beautiful man she had ever seen in her life, a complete stranger whom she never saw in her life, but he felt very familiar her like she seen his face before, but where, either way, this very tall stranger, that has jet black hair looking like someone she should be afraid of, instead of Steven, with his black leather jacket, a tight white t, with loose faded jeans and black biker boots was her savior, she didn't care what he looked like she really grateful to him.

Steven continued to groan in pain with his arm pinned against his back and his face smashed into the counter "Who the fuck are you?" Steve huffed trying to get air into his lungs to speak to the handsome stranger. The stranger leaned over Steven crushing him further into the counter cutting off his air making it hard for Steve to speak let alone to breathe, letting Steve and everyone around this stranger, know that he meant business he wasn't backing down one bit "I am your worst nightmare coming true someone who hates would be rapists, I am about to bust some heads!" the stranger threatened.

"Hey, pal I am no rapist the Bitch was asking for it!" Steven snapped back "oh my bad let's ask her then, shall we!" then the stranger with a look of kindness in his dark brown eyes along with the look of concern at her.

She blinked at him trying to read his silence message to her "Love, did you give this fucker, sorry, permission to touch you?' Then water began to pool in her blue eyes Sabrina leaned over to look the man dead in his kind eyes with her chin trembling making her answer crystal clear to the stranger and the other men, she answered back "Hell, no!!".

With a soft nod of his head at the lovely young waitress, Jack turns his attention back toward the fucker Jack still held his face firmly on the counter than leaned over him "There she said no!" Jack answered back to the mother fucker "the Bitch is a waitress she has been asking for it!" Steve groans loudly trying to continue to breath harder trying hard to get air into his lungs. Jack didn't like that response Jack reapplied leaning further on the fucker's back causing more pain "I don't give a fuck if she is a lady of the night when a woman says no, she means it!" Jack gritted his teeth.

From the corner of his eye, Jack sees a movement from behind him, the tall friend was moving toward him. Jack quickly grabbed his switchblade knife he hid in his back pocket of his jeans. Jack quickly jabbed the blade through the mother fucker's the solid circle end of his silver chain linked, necklace causing the links to tighten up cutting off his air further causing him to choke, Steve tried to get loose, but the beautiful stranger was too quick on his feet, gave Steve's tall friend a hard gab to his middle section causing Mr. Tall to bend in half and then groan in pain, like Steve, the beautiful stranger face planted Mr. Tall on the counter "well looks like your friend is trying to be a hero, not smart friend" the stranger gritted his teeth at them.

Then Sabrina felt Mr. Chubby hands let go of her, saw him from the corner of her eye come toward the stranger, fearing for his life when he was trying to save her, she quickly grabs a glass pop bottle that was beside her hand she whacks Mr. Chubby hard on his head sending shard of broken glass everywhere and saw the look of shock Mr. Chubby on his face, he clasps to the floor, like a rag doll.

Then the handsome stranger looks at her with a smirk of pride mouthed, thank you to her for helping him then asked, "Shall I take out the trash for you maim?" trying to force a grin on her lovely face "please do. Thank you!" she answered back "No, problem!" he answered with a wink and beautiful smile on his handsome face.

Jack grabs both the sandy hair man and the tall friend by their collars almost dragging them to their feet tossing them out the Diner door into the parking lot. Then march back into the Diner coming toward Mr. Chubby still lying on the floor out cold by Sabrina. Jack grabs the back of the collar of the big guy's jean jacket then grabbing the back of the waistband of his jeans picking him up like he did the other bastards. Then Sabrina asked the handsome stranger "is he dead?" with a concerned look on her face.

The handsome stranger with a kind looks on his face answered back "no darling, he will have one hell of a headache thou." He picks up Mr. Chubby by the collar and back of the waistband from his jeans, dragging him to the glass door and pushing him out through the door into the parking lot and kicking him in thee ass.

Sabrina sighed with relief and slides down the side corner of the counter began to circle up in a ball trying to be as small as possible began to snob uncontrollable as the shock of the horror of about what might have happened to her sets in, if the handsome stranger didn't show up when he did.

Then she heard heavy boot steps coming toward where she was hiding and felt his warm presence kneeling beside her. Then placing a warm, gentle hand on her shoulder trying sooth her pain, in a deep, soft voice barely a whisper, the handsome stranger "Hey Love, are you alright?" ask her, Jack fearing the worse might have happen before he got there.

Sabrina sobbed shaking her head with answering him and mumbled a soft, "no" with sniffles "do you want me to take you to the hospital?" the stranger asked again trying to figure out how to solve her suffering "No thank you I am fine, physically." she answered softly, back looking at her fingers and with her legs still circled up.

Then she circled her arms around herself trying to ward off the eerie chill that had entered her body that caused her to tremble a little. "Do you have a family or a friend I can take you too?" Jack asked softly trying to figure out how to help this poor woman that needed help he didn't know how to help he had never come face to face with trouble like this thou he has seen people treat others in a wrong way, broke up fights here and there. He didn't know how to help a woman who needs emotional support, that family or friends that can provide.

The first time, in a long time Sabrina felt the loneliness that she had her whole life come rushing towards her, this was when she truly needed someone the most to comfort her, to have someone out in the world that actually cares for her because they care, she had no one " I have no one here" Sabrina began to sob more uncontrollable this time, then a miracle happened "well, you know what you have me, let's get you to the back office, okay."

The beautiful stranger gentle scooped her up like she was a small helpless child "Place your arms around my neck" he softly soothed , but order her to do she welcomed the support this perfect stranger offered her, as he carried her off toward the kitchen area where the door toward the office was which surprised her that he knew where the office was without asking her she didn't care all she was concerned with, was someone was looking after her needs for once.

She felt like she was that small helpless little girl again when everything she knew back then had changed for her when father left, when every man she has come across as done her wrong, her stepfather, Jared and now Steve, but this stranger was different towards her, something new he showed her true kindness something she wasn't use to this kind of attention, but she was grateful for it and she will cherish it.

CHAPTER 6

Sabrina sobbed uncontrollably while his perfect, but very handsome stranger who held her while lying on the old, rugged, ugly orange and yellow couch, the hot, sexy stranger continued to sooth the sorrow offering some support to Sabrina, with his strong arms wrapped around her, she felt safe for the first time, in his black leather jacket he patiently allow her to cry until she was finished it felt forever to him, when finally she softly spoke up, "I can't believe he wanted to do to me what he wanted to do to me, Steve always treated me like I was shit to kick around, but I never thought he wanted to, Oh god!" Sabrina began to bawl her eyes out.

She stopped herself from completing that sentence trying to wrap her mind around that thought caused her, to cry some more then she realized that she was with a complete stranger whom she was eternally grateful to, this handsome stranger who saved her from a horrifying fate than death.

She suddenly became very aware of his presence felt the warmth, the hard muscled body through his white cotton t-shirt cover, she felt her own body come alive just merely laying there she leans up looking at his very breathtaking face his smooth, chiseled chin, his skin was copper, his eyebrows were thick that shaped his eyes nicely he took care of himself she didn't know what he did for a living to acquire for him, to look after himself, did she want to know with how he took care of Steve and his Goons by himself.

Sabrina felt her eyes come to rest on his beautiful mouth that she assumed as given more women pleasures, she wondered how those lips would feel on her body if she knew him better instead, she was laying there with him adding comfort to her, she shook her head, what was wrong with her. She was thinking about sex when she was almost raped it was like her body wasn't her friend right now.

Sabrina was straddling his long legs she looks down at him trying to figure out what do or say to this stranger, his face was so beautiful to her, she was wondering where he came from why was he there, his jet black hair feathered around framing his handsome face, she wanted to run her fingers through it to see if his hair was as soft as it looked to her.

She felt this delicious warm tingle rush through her again as they continue to lay on this old rugged yellow and orange flower fabric covered couch that was in the office of the Diner that housed the fresh vegetables, the other food supplies, the lockers for the employees, and Alan's desk in the center of the room.

Jack gazed up at the beautiful face of the angel that was straddling his legs right now he liked the warmth of her lovely body that was wrapped up in her cute little waitress uniform as she layed in his arms, Jack tried to comfort and ease her pain.

Jack was grateful when he showed up, he didn't want to think if he was few minutes late, he would have killed the blonde mother fucker, this beautiful woman would have been through the worse than death, she was there in his arms right now crying in shock with what might have happened if he didn't, he didn't want to think about the what if part.

"Are you all, right?" he asks softly breaking the silence "Yeah I am fine, thank you." She whispered back with a shy smile on her face, looking at him she wrapped her arms around herself trying to ward off the eerie chili that creeped inside her thinking about that what if too.

Jack placed his hands on her arms running them up and down trying to help her warm herself up he thought it was more from the shock, he hoped.

"Hey, let's close this bird down, I will take you home. What do you say?" he asked softly "I would love to, but I can't I am not the owner of this place they would freak if they knew I closed down early, I don't want to call them." "Well, you know what I will give the go-ahead to lock up. okay?" he said with a smirk.

Sabrina looks at him in confusion, blinking at him like he was crazy, but then she looked at the side wall of the office behind the hard dark oak desk, with the matching chair on wheels. The side wall that has the old black and white photos of Julia and Alan when they were younger, when they first got married, their young family gathered on fishing trips, in front of the diner when the Diner was first opened, then Sabrina's eyes rested on a large photo of a young guy that had the same kind black eyes and handsome face that was lying beneath her at the moment then she smiled at him with a soft giggle "You look like your Father" she said softly with a shy smile.

"I do?" Jack asks back when he glanced at the photo she was looking at "Oh you do, no wonder why I felt like I knew you, but I didn't know where until I looked at that picture of you just now on the wall".

Jack leans back looking at the same picture that Sabrina was looking at "that was my graduation picture before things changed." wanting to ask further what he meant, but didn't want to press him it was between him and his folks, not her " your folks have talked about you so much I feel like I know you," "I bet" he answered with the same smirk on his handsome face.

Sabrina slowly climbs off of him "did you want something to eat I am sure you are hungry from wherever you came from." She looks back at him as he got off the couch to follow her toward the office door that leads back through the kitchen back through the swing lobby door. "California" Jack answered her "what?' she asked wondering what he meant about California, "oh that, was where I came from, I just ended a year-long concert tour, sweetheart what is your name by the way?" he asked, giving her a breathtaking smile.

"Oh, I am Sabrina Parker," she answered back offering her hand to him. Jack takes her small soft hand into his large, rough, gentle hands, both feeling the same delicious tingle racing through their vanes "I am Jack Taylor" he answered back "Hi Jack nice to finally meet you, just wished it was under better circumstances" she said as she glanced down at the lobby floor sadly and shyly taking back her hand to place it on her left arm to ward off the brief chill thinking about the nightmare that almost happened with Steve "hey are you sure you are okay?" as Jack places his hand on her shoulder to comfort her some more "I will be, thank you" she smiled back at Jack. "You know you are not alone in this; we can call my parents to let them know what happened" Jack with concern look and tone in his voice "no, no unless you want to surprise them to let them know that you are here?" she offered a small smile trying to forget what happened earlier.

S abrina and Jack were now standing outside the diner that was shut down; besides Jack's Arch bike, he climbs on first getting the bike ready for her to climb behind him. He offered his hand to her then she looks at the hand wondering how it would feel on her, but then quickly squashed that thought from her mind then quickly took his hand feeling the warmth and strength it provided her in her time of need she was grateful towards Jack, he could have easily walked away from her, but choice to fight for her without even knowing her, when her own flesh and blood just walked away from her without giving her a second thought that meant a lot to her, as she straddles his bike placing her hands on the sides of his leather jacket that he wore "No darling I want you safe while riding with me, okay." Jack grabs her hands placing them around him on his hard abs even through his white t-shirt she felt his warmth causing her mouth to go dry, Sabrina felt herself lose her senses while sitting on his bike.

Jack caressed the back of her hand she had the softest skin he had ever felt in a long time causing his cock to tighten a little making his loose jeans become uncomfortable, he wondered how it would be if he took things farther with Sabrina would she scream and moan his name, with his face between her beautiful long legs with what she almost went through he would be no worse than that fucker that tried to force himself on her and he didn't want her to see him that way not until she gave him her permission to do so.

Sabrina closed her eyes for a moment, breathing in the scent of this hunky man sitting in front of her on his bike, his scent was musky, with hint of the outdoors, the leather jacket, Jack's personal scent caused her blood to warm further putting her head into the clouds "here output these on, please." Jack offered Sabrina some sunglasses to protect her lovely eyes from the sun breaking the spell she was so near him " sorry I don't carry extra helmets for you to wear unless you want to use mine, I promise to keep you safe, trust me." Sabrina smiled at him "it's okay" answered back, getting all giddy ,with the ride that she was about to get on, with this rock god that millions of his female fan would kill her for, to her he was the most beautiful, perfect man that she had ever meet who was her Hero.

"Ready?" Jack asked her "ready" she answered back,

with a large grin on her face as she nodded at him, giving him a quick hug touching him deeply.

Jack rolls his bike back, stirring it toward the entrance leading away from the Diner this time heading out towards one of Jack's favorite places. Jack jumps starts the engine causing the bike to roar back to life again. "Heading out toward the highway" from Jack's radio was playing.

Feeling the warmth from the gulf breeze that played with anything that it touched Sabrina loved the warmth from the falling sun on her skin, but trying to keep her favorite soft, pink sweater on her shoulders from the wind was a gift given to her from her long-lost father that she found living in Midnight a few miles away where his hotel resort called the Charleston was located, at the other end of Midnight, right now she riding on Jack's bike she didn't want to think about anything else except for Jack, as they continue to ride along the road that lines the coast below them where the rugged cliffs, the white sandy beaches this was heaven to her, she prayed that this moment would last forever.

Jack placed his large hand over hers causing Sabrina to look at him through the side mirror on his Arch. The small touches, the kind jesters were affecting her more than he would ever know that she wished she could tell him that she was afraid to let him in, that he might think she wasn't worth the risk, getting close to her, she would keep quiet for now someday she would have to reveal all to him "hey your quiet, everything okay?" he shouted through the wind so she could hear him "Yes

I am fine, thank you!" Sabrina shouted through her smile "Love, you're not to tire to take a walk with me?" he shouted back and pointing toward a small private beach that was on the right as they just passed a large box style very modern beach house that faced the gulf what a view this house has, she envies anyone who owned it "No! I am not tired answered back.

Jack slows his bike, stirs towards a lookout a mile past the beach house, he parks on the gravel lookout, with the white sandy beach below, that he was referring to when he pointed toward it earlier in the ride.

Sabrina looks off towards the water was in awe of the power of the waves, the wind as they raced, beating torturing the cliffs by slamming against them just below the lookout, Sabrina was standing on, closing her eyes loving the sounds that the waves were making. She smiled at the squawking seagulls flying above her if they were putting on a small performance making her feel she had died and gone to heaven if this what heaven look like she didn't want it to end.

Sabrina would stand on her balcony and long to be at the beach to bury her feet to feel the cool gritty sand against her skin, but she was so busy and poor to take any time off to enjoy the beaches even thou this is where she chose to come to hide from her past to rebuild her life over but never did until now thanks to, again to the beautiful man who was slowly come up to her.

Jack looked out toward the sea "Before I left Midnight to start my music career I would come here to play my guitar or to clear my head, this place was where I made the decision that I wanted to be a rock star." he said telling her how this beach meant to him, Sabrina was touched that he would share this special place with her, she wished she could share a beautiful memory with him like he was with her.

Sabrina would always remember this moment for the rest of her life, she wanted to thank him somehow, but not yet. "When I get home at night, I sometimes would stand on my balcony and hear the calmness of the waters rushing toward the sand and the rocks. I couldn't wait to bury my feet in the sand and feel the coolness of the waters!" She smiles a little with a blush then looks away from him, "but never had the chance to do so".

"I sound like a silly schoolgirl, don't I?" she said shyly. "Nope!" he smiled back to her than offered her his hand "Well, Miss Parker, would you care to walk down toward the beach so you can feel the sand on your sexy feet" Jack said with a smile causing her to blush a little, she gladly took his hand and said, "I would love too! Thank you!" forgetting the sexy feet part like he was joking, no one has ever told her she was sexy not even her feet.

Jack takes Sabrina by the hand carefully, leading her down the long flight of stairs that lead down to the sandy white beach below. While they were making their way down the stairs Sabrina would glance at the private beach loving the beautiful scenery before her watching the waves crashing against the sandy ground and against the jagged cliffs that half curved around the beach, watching the seagulls circling above Jack and Sabrina, like they were clumsy dancers continuing their show, she was truly in awe of it like her worries were gone, thanks to Jack.

Jack and Sabrina finally touched the sandy ground with their shoes, Sabrina looks toward the beach, the endless water feeling like she was a little girl who got the greatest gift ever.

Sabrina closed her eyes again for a moment as she allows the wind to play with her long blonde hair and her clothes, she couldn't believe she was on a beach finally, she loves the beach she only lived near man-made beaches, not nature made.

Sabrina looks down at the skirt of her waitress uniform crunched down to take off her heels and hose, when a pair of strong hands moved her hands out of the way, Jack began to undo the buckle on her high heels and then taking her shoe off her foot.

Sabrina breath caught in her throat as she felt his long fingers crawl up the skirt of her waitress uniform to slowly peel off her nylon hose her leg and foot, her breath caught in her throat from his touch as he caressed almost touching her mound where her long legs came together thank god for her white cotton panties he would be touching her flesh instead, she did want his touch, or didn't she was getting confused about her sudden attraction towards Jack, she didn't think he was aware of what he was doing, 'he was being a gentleman' she was telling herself.

"God, he is so beautiful!" Sabrina thought, he was

so tall and muscular in all the right places, his jeans were loose, but fit his very nice ass not that she notices.

Then she realized that Jack was watching her too taking her breath away, making her heartbeat faster as she studied his face for a moment admiring the strong chin lines, his straight nose that curved down making him look his Indian heritage right now, but his dark to almost black eyes seemed to warm right through her like he was looking into her heart and soul. Sabrina was happy that she was sitting right now because she would have melted right there with this beautiful man would seeing the less graceful part of her.

When Sabrina quickly looked away, breaking the spell totally ignoring the strong pull that Jack was having on her that warmed her to the core of her.

The feelings Sabrina was having for Jack felt wrong to her, she couldn't trust Jack right now thou he did show her that she could. Sabrina needed to be cautious with Jack, thanks to her past who can't let her forget.

Sabrina sheepishly smiled at Jack, politely thanked him for his help with her shoes and hose, trying hard to forget how close his fingers were to her pussy.

Jack gave her the warmest smile while still kneeling before her, helping her with her shoes his hand was at the hem of her hose as she felt the silky fabric being peeled down her long legs feeling the cool the breeze and the warmth of Jack's hand.

She didn't know what thrilled her the most Jack or the air, maybe a little both "I know I should be put off by this special attention that Jack was giving me." She thought of Jared.

Sabrina wanted to trust Jack he seemed trustworthy, she kept quiet to see what he did next when he took her hose off, he gave each her feet a massage, then took her heels along with her hose placing them behind a large black boulder that was sticking up from the sand that surrounds it.

Jack then quickly took off his boots and socks, placing them beside her shoes too.

Jack walks towards Sabrina than offered his hand to her, "Ready beautiful" he asked without thinking twice Sabrina gladly took his hand, but was stunned when he called her beautiful, she didn't know what to say to that, so she ignored it, as they began to walk down toward the water.

"So, tell me beautiful what are you doing here in Midnight? Darling, where are you from?" Jack asked as they strolled down the length of the beach, watching the waves crashing against the sand toward them, the wind playing with their skin and their clothes.

Sabrina looks up at Jack pondering rather or not to tell him the truth about why she came here to Midnight to escape her ex-boyfriend Jared who is still out there looking for her, she hoped and prayed that he would never trance her here destroying everything that she had worked so hard to rebuild. "I loved the water there aren't a lot of beaches in Idaho where I am from." Sabrina told a half-truth to him then looked down at their hands holding each other, amazed at how comfortable this was, she couldn't tell which fingers were hers which ones were his like they were one.

This felt different to her, it was comfortable to her like it was supposed to be normal she didn't know have anything to compare it to, she always had to be on guard with men, but not with Jack he made her feel wanted, valued like her needs mattered to him.

Sabrina smiled to herself, she was excited being with this amazing man walking beside her, holding her hand, as they continue to talk about this and that, getting to know one another, wondering to each other what the future held for them if there was a future.

Sabrina asks Jack more about his music career, admitting that she never heard of his songs expect through the jukebox she loved music, like country, rock, mostly music with a little heart in it.

Sabrina went on to explain how she fell in love with music through her grandmother though she never meet her mother's mom because she had already passed away when she was a baby, she did hear her mother talk about a trip to the mountains that her mother and father took in New Kirk, they owned a cabin up in the mountains there.

How her grandmother would pretend that she was directing invisible choir while she looked out on a cliff that looks out toward the valley below, she wasn't quiet or in tune when she would sing, most of the time, her grandfather would shout to her to knock that racket off she was scaring the game away. Sabrina smiled at the only happy memory that she can remember from her childhood she had with her mother which sadden her because her happy memories are few and far between, some included her parents when they were still together, but she barely remembers that time. When her mother was clean and sober, trying to live a good life.

"Are you okay?" Jack asked softly when he saw the sad look come over her face like a dark cloud coming across her lovely face, then disappear like never it happened, which worried him thinking it was the attack, but his gut was telling him that there was something more that she wasn't telling.

Sabrina looked up at Jack wondering if would be okay to tell him the truth about her life, but feared if he knew what her life was like he would not look at her in the same way, she decided to keep quiet about her paste she knows someday he would know the truth about her, she was worried what his reaction would be, who was she kidding she wasn't perfect ask her stepfather, she decided at that moment not reveal too much of herself until she felt she could trust Jack with the truth right now she couldn't trust anyone "yeah I am fine thank you for your concern.

As they continue their walk on the beach "see that house up there on that ridge?" as he pointed to the same beach house that they passed to get to this beach. "Yes?" she answered back "what about it?" "What do you think?" he asked, wanting her opinion hoping that she liked it. "I think, wow, what a house, but not really my style thou, but I envy the person who has to look at that every morning!" as Sabrina points to the open waters. Jack smiled at the compliment but wondered what she thought if she knew that the house was his, that he bought before he arrived back in Texas.

Just then a large wave crashed into the would-be lovers, Jack, clasps Sabrina by the shoulders trying to keep them from falling to the sand.

Sabrina looks up at Jack when he leans in than Sabrina places her hands on the front of his leather jacket getting caught up in an unbreakable spell surrounding them in the beauty of the ocean.

The crystal white sand, the tall dark castle-like cliffs keeping them safe from onlookers, the deep blue waters of the Gulf continue to rush towards them while they stand there on the beach looking at each other. Jack slowly lowers his lips onto Sabrina soft inviting mouth not feeling any protests from her he continues deepening the kiss with his tongue caressing inside her mouth he never tasted anything sweeter or addicting then any drink he had ever before.

Sabrina slides her arms around Jack's neck bring him down closer trying to make the kiss last longer than Jack slid his hands up and down her beautiful body, sliding them down toward her ass cupping a feel enjoying the feel of her soft, warm petite body along with her tight ass.

A tiny gasp escaped from Sabrina when Jack gently lifted her leaving her feet dangled in the air. Sabrina felt like she was floating on air even if a small part of her should feel offended by the assault on her mouth along with her ass by being cupped by Jack's hands, but she didn't want the moment to end she never felt such hunger or warmth in one kiss with everyone especially with someone she barely knew. As long as she lives, she will never forget this first kiss and she will be forever grateful to him.

Jack then placed Sabrina back on the sand as if on cue another wave rushed onto the sand crashing into them causing them to separate quickly. They continue to stare at each other for a moment wondering what to do next.

Sabrina felt a bit reckless a little wanton wanting another kiss she leaned up, but Jack feeling bit more cautious how he was treating this woman before him a moment which wasn't fair to her after all she was almost raped, he wanted to take things slow with Sabrina treat her like a lady that she was instead of a whore like how he used to treat women before her, he quickly stopped her by firmly holding her shoulders at arm length, but not hard enough to cause any pain, he could see a confused look on her face.

Jack took Sabrina hand in his, trying to convey a silenced message her, they needed to slow things down. "Let's walk some more, there is a cave up the way I want you to see." He said, leading them toward the secluded cove surrounded by the cliffs above the jagged rocks that gave a very intimate feel in case someone wanted to do more private things without anyone seeing, it felt cozy and private.

Sabrina felt so confused and a little hurt she wanted that second kiss but got the total brush off, then all her insecurities came rushing over her, she felt embarrassed thinking he wanted more, he was the one that stopped the kiss from happening maybe her lack of experience with men was coming through loud and clear to him, she didn't know "what was I thinking anyway." she chided herself as she turned toward the waters as she watched the waves churning rushing toward the beach.

She closed her eyes, forcing the silent tears to stop, that threatened to come down her cheeks she didn't want this almost romantic moment to end with this perfect stranger that she knew nothing about except from the stories that his parents told her about.

Then suddenly a chill began to engulf her causing her to rub her sweater-clad arms than she felt Jack's leather jacket come around her shoulders to help warm her up a little she stiffens up a little as he warms up her arms she didn't want him to see her weakness and awkwardness.

Sabrina lowered her guard down a little she leaned into him welcoming the warmth, the comfort he was providing her for the moment even thou he didn't know that inner turmoil she was struggling with "Hey, are you okay darling? Do you want to leave?" Jack asked with a concerned look on his face as he watched the storm clouds come across her beautiful angel face then disappear again as if they were never there.

Sabrina studies Jack's handsome face admiring the straight, eagle nose that he got from his father and mother, along with his father's square strong jawline, his lips were amazing a full bottom, a thinner top she could still feel the imprint they left on her mouth she wanted more from him, she afraid she might have scared him off so she decided to play this cool while he was still here in Texas.

"Are you okay?" Jack asked when her deep blue eyes looked at him a half smile came across her lovely mouth "Yes, I am fine thanking you for your concern, I appreciate it. "She answered back but didn't answer further leaving the question to be answered later.

"Did you want to sit to watch the waves with me for a bit, or do you want to go?" He asks hoping she would answer his silent plead to stay to watch the waves with him so they could prolong their time together, as if she could read him "No I would love to watch the waves, I don't know when I would get another chance, it's so breathtaking here." As she stands with her arms folded watching the water as if on cue a big wave crashed into the sand racing toward them covering their feet causing ice cold shivers racing through them.

Jack took her by the arm with his hand guiding her toward the blanket. Sabrina wonders how it got there, she didn't remember Jack carrying it with them, they walked further into the cove away from the water.

Sabrina knelt down on the blanket as she used her hands to whip away the extra sand that gathered on the red and black checkered wool blanket spreading it further. She then turned while still kneeling to face the waves than plopped onto the old blanket as she stretched her legs than she wrapped her arms around her knees, she felt the warmth of Jack's presence and his hard chest causing her to get light headed and breathless at the same time she took a deep breath smelling his sandalwood and spicey cologne along with his own masculine scent making her heart to beat faster. She never felt so attracted toward someone she just met, there was something unfamiliar she never felt before safe maybe a little cherished or she was reading too much into this.

Sabrina did feel comfortable in his arms, a little too comfortable that scared her, but she didn't want to come across rude or unappreciated for what he was showing or offering, so she gave in began to relax, to drift off to sleep, still wrapped in his amazing arms "Hey, are you fallen asleep on me?" Jack whispered softly to her causing her to open her eyes "yes, sorry." She answered back "It's okay, why don't you close those beautiful eyes and sleep. We can spend the night here. I know the owner he won't mind." Jack circled the collar of his leather jacket around the sweet neck of hers "Okay, thank you" she answered shyly than she snuggled her beautiful face against his neck still looking up at him "God he is beautiful" she thought to herself what it would be like to have him all to herself, if he gave her half a chance, God she hoped so. She felt herself drifting off again, this time she was out. Jack placed his mouth on her forehead placing a soft kiss "Night, my sweet Angel" he whispered, "Hmm, night." She whispered back.

Jack carried the sleeping beauty in his arms into the house that stood on the ridge that looked over the sea below.

CHAPTER 8

Sabrina woke up with a start she wasn't on the sandy beach anymore, the last time she remembered, instead she was in a bright, but a dim lite room everything around her was really white and serene, the walls were all white with small framed photos of bright colored daisies there four pictures above the headboard of the bed she was in, even the linens were white this felt like a dream, but it wasn't, Sabrina pinched herself encase she was dreaming or worse "No I am alive, thank god!", then soft muted sounds of water or waves coming crashing, outside the room she was along with the calling of gulls.

Sabrina slowly climbed out of the bed she was in she looked down at herself she noticed she wasn't in her waitress uniform anymore she looked around the room to see were her uniform was it was gone, she was in her white very thin slip she felt a rush of panic, one she doesn't remember how she got here and now she is almost naked except for her slip and panties thank god she felt relief rush over her as she felt the faint line of her panties through her slip.

Sabrina didn't know who she should be mad at, the person who brought here or herself for allowing her guard down when she swore that she would never do that again she was alive and safe, she is grateful so she wasn't upset she needed to set some ground rules with Mr. Taylor who was absent right now she wondered were he disappear too and why did he leave her here she was not happy with him and again with her, but the waves outside were calling her.

Then she looked at the large panoramic window giving her a picturisk of the waves below her, she was in awe of the waves crashing into the rugged black cliffs, the gulf was alive the skies were blue and bright with a hint of clouds the view before her was a picturisk if she had a camera she would have captured it, she looked around her to find something to cover herself when her eyes came to rest on the fluffy white robe that laid across the foot of the bed that she was in. She quickly grabs the robe circling it around her while putting on her, wanting a closer look outside. She went to the balcony door opening it, she instantly felt the wind blowing and the warmth of the morning sun caressing her skin. She could taste the salty air on her lips and moisture on her skin, she looked around her trying to remember how she got here and/or by whom.

Then her memory of last night how Jack points out the beach house that looked too modern to her, but she loved the location she envied the person would own this place who had to face this every morning as if whomever it was since her envy wanted her to experience what they faced every morning when they woke up. She breathed in the warm salty air, loving what they had to face and what a shame she smiled to herself.

Then the sound of metal pan crashing to the floor caused her to jump. She looks into the direction the sound came from then she went in search of the person who owns the house she was guessing it was the familiar stranger she just met last night.

Frankie's Witchcraft voice say 'you have put a spell on me' from the state of art sound system that flooded through the living area that had an opened floor to the ceiling with a countertop that divided the kitchen from living room with a white overstuffed couch and dark glass inlay wood squared coffee table that faced the couch that lined the beach house's large bay windows. She looked around her there was a black inserted fireplace that was surrounded by white marble and white-walled bookcases that housed some books other things like trophies that were won a long time ago, the sound system, the flat screen looked like a movie screen was above the fireplace.

Sabrina heard continual movement coming from the kitchen she moved toward the countertop what she saw was every woman fantasized when they woke up every morning having really a hot good looking guy with a sculpted chest and arms covered in a short sleaved, pale blue t, the lower half wearing only dark blue and black p.j. bottoms that hung so nicely off his hips giving that hot and sexy vibe making Sabrina lose her breath, her mouth water wanting to know what was below those pants has she spies the dark hair narrow down his happy trail.

Jack felt her presence he turned to look at her from the kitchen sink that had a picture framed window that looked out toward the cliffs of his house that he just bought before he came to Texas.

Jack turns to look at the beautiful woman that was still clad in her barely-there slip and the fluffy white robe that he placed on the bed in one his guest bedrooms when he carried her in, she fell asleep in his arms as they watched the waves last night, he didn't have the heart to wake her to take her home.

"Morning, beautiful" Jack greeting the beautiful creature before him, she looks at him, he gave her a soul-piercing look instead of frightening her, it warmed her blood like she was the most desirable woman in the world to him, her long blonde hair was a mess she was still clad in her barely-there white slip that ran the length of her slender body above the knees along with the white bathrobe he placed on the bed for her to wear at the foot of the bed when he carried her in last night, he walks slowly to her, stalking her, towering over her as if she is a delicious prey that is there for him to slowly devour he couldn't wait to taste every inch of her. He grabs her by the shoulders gently brings her closer, so she was fleshed to him causing her to gasp, he placed his hands on the side of her slender neck enjoying the feel of her soft, warm skin and silky hair.

Sabrina felt the warmth of his touch on her skin, she wondered to herself what it would feel like on the rest of her body, that hunger for his touch, his hands were on the side of her neck was caressing the lines of her chin, sending delicious warm, feverish shivers coursing through her veins, warming her blood to the core of her making her want more. Cutting off any protest or speech she might have made at that moment, to his greeting, he placed his lips on hers causing her to gasp, a little he wrapped his arms her trying to deepen the kiss.

The second kiss they shared since they had met, in the last few hours felt like they known each other forever, but this kiss was taking her breath away with their tongues dancing caressing like they were one body breathing for each other, soft and hungry.

Jack slid his hands down the length of her beautiful body Jack knew some models would kill to have, he loved her beautiful mouth was soft and warm, delicious everything he thought they were.

Jack's continued to caress her body with his hands, when they slid down passed her small waist, finding her cute little, but firm ass causing her to smile a little while they continued their make-out session in the kitchen, Jack cups her lovely ass lifting her up causing her to wrap her long arms around his neck with her long beautiful legs wrapped around his waist, causing his cock to harden with the rest of his hard body responding.

Jack carries Sabrina through the opening she entered from the living room to the kitchen while they continue their kissing. Then he places her gently on the bar stool that lined the counter that curved around the small kitchen for a big house. "House guess on this side of the line." He ordered "Do you always greet your house guest so friendly" she flirted back "No just you" he teased back he winked flashing her a smile "Oh so I am special then." She answered back "oh you are very special, my dear" He flirted sounding more sexier causing some pink color to rise in her cheeks giving him a shy look.

"What if the house guest wants to cook your dinner or breakfast or clean your house even." She asked "My house my rules" he answered "you break my rules I will put you over my knee and spank that lovely behind of yours" "is that so?" she purred back him "Yep" he flirted back as he tucked a loose strand of silk paled blonde hair behind her right ear caress the side of her cheek with the side of his left thumb sending those delicious shivers down her body.

Then he looks at the beautiful lips that he tasted a moment ago he hungers for them again cutting off any protest or speech again, he placed his hand on the back of her head looking at her with such hunger throwing any caution he had before out the window because he wanted more.

Jack could tell by the kiss that she gave him she wanted more too why was he so turned on by this beautiful angel sitting on the stool he places her on to keep her out of his kitchen, with her angel face, cat-like dark blue eyes saw right through him, he continued to caress the inside of her tasting, of chocolate, honey, with a hint of strawberries sweet mouth.

Jack pulled back ending the mind-blowing kiss he couldn't wait to taste the rest of her, he needed to be patient with her thou she was willing to give what her body wanted, they needed to slow things down before they crashed this thing into the ground before they got started, they both wanted this thing to last whatever this thing was?

"What do you want for breakfast, my love." He walks around her walking toward the kitchen just stopped at the entrance to hear her request. Sabrina leans up against the counter looking at the true beauty of this man that seemed perfect in every way except for his extreme bossiness that irritated her, delighted her in the same way, but she needed to let him know that she wasn't going to be controlled by anyone not even him even if he was her boss because he owned part of the diner, this mystery feeling she was having toward Jack, was getting stronger by the moment that shock her, she wonder why at this time when she been looking for love or something like it, when she thought that she had given up that part of her life because she rather be a lone and single, then with someone who was mean, cruel and selfish, but here she was with someone who could be everything that she dislikes in a guy, but no Jack is the total opposite then what she had before with Jared where he was the perfect All American boy with the blonde and icy blue eyes that oozed charm he blinded her with gifts and attention, looking back on her life with Jared it was negative he would tell her what he liked if she gave her opinion he didn't like it, he spoiled her at first convinced her that he loved her, she was the only one in his life for him, but when things got serious with her slowly his perfect persona began to grumble around her when she slowly found out the real reason he hooked up with her in the first place not because he loved her no he was using her, because she worked at one the top banks in New Kirk that housed the accounts of the very wealthy peeps that did business and lived in New Kirk.

Sabrina looked at her life at the time, she was so stupid and naive back then, she looks at the man in the kitchen who was looking at her with a small smile. "Hey, darling are you all right, your awfully quiet there?" Jack with a look of concern on his handsome face, she wishes she could trust him enough to tell him that she wasn't okay inside. She was a hot mess and afraid of what he would think of her if he knew the truth about her that she wasn't this perfect angel if he needs the real her inside.

Jack reaches over the counter placing his warm, strong hand that could crush a single man into bits onto hers, but this touch was gentle and caring instead of being frightening which she should have been, she was touched. But she didn't want to scare him away he could be the best guy she ever had in her life she didn't want to give him up just yet. She looks up placing a fake smile on her face "I am fine, thank you." She lied.

Jack looks at her, she was hiding something he could tell with how quiet she was and evasive the next without saying much like avoiding the truth, but he isn't going to push until she is ready to spill. He is patient he will wait for the answers until then he will enjoy the ride with Sabrina.

The smoke from cigarette billowed as Jared look out the window of his black 57 Camaro his pride and joy, he wished he was laying on a beach chair sunning himself with a bale of beauties that were clad in bikinis of all kinds of blonde, Burnett, and redheads waiting on him instead he is sitting here baking to death in this godforsaken desert that surrounds him is empty and dry. Kind of like how He feels nothing at the moment waiting for the dam payphone to ring from the detective he hired to trace, tracked down the little bitch who put a stopped to his plans and dreams of being filthy rich.

Sabrina showed him the evidence she had found at his place, of him stealing money and account information, then the payphone began to ring causing him to smile "Hey, what's up, what do you have, you're sure? Really, she did say she loved the beach, well Texas here I come!" Jared chuckled taking another drag of his cigar as the smoke billowed out the car window then started the engine stirring off toward the highway.

Jack dropped off Sabrina at *the diner* he was too scared to meet his folks face to face "come on Jack get it together, you didn't come all this way home to turn back now." That he chided himself for being a chicken shit, then he turns walks toward the glass door, grabbing the handle walks in sees the beautiful angel face that he dropped off earlier looking up to see him, with a bright smile spreading across that lovely face of hers making him forget for a moment why he came back the second time, she was taking some customers order when he came in he walks towards her "Hi" he breathed he wanted to continue to stare at this lovely creature that stood before him, but he needed to see his parents first why he road all the way back to Midnight in the first place, but he didn't except to run into the non-delegable Sabrina with her sparkling blue eyes, pale skin soft as a baby skin, plus the killer curves causing his body to harden especially his cock, he again knew a few models that would kill to have her figure including her skin, with her beautiful smile that lite up her whole face in fact she lite up the whole fucking room to him.

Sabrina continues to smile at him then places her small hand on his chest imprinting its warmth on his skin and soul even through his chest covered in his white t-shirt. Jack would give anything to be alone with her again, but this time he would be kissing her from head to toe tasting her drowning himself in her, with his face between her legs while he took his time drinking in her sweet juices, he gave a little-teased of her at his beach house, he wanted more will get more soon if he can help it from this incredible woman facing him with a small smile on her face.

Hi" Sabrina answered back with the same whisper, stepping away from her customers she was helping, with a smile still on her face, looking at this amazing man standing before her with his well-worn out blue jeans loosed fitted that fit him very well that hang off his muscled hips just fine, his white t-shirt that fitted his chest like it was seconded skin wearing his signature black leather jacket. She could sense Jack was a little nervous, he told her the real reason why he came to Midnight was to heal the rip he caused with his parents when he left after he graduated school.

Sabrina placed her hand on his rock-hard chest feeling every muscle move causing her to lose her train of thought, she wanted to give him some encouraging word, some kind of support or whatever he needed to help him to make the first step bearable, her head at the moment was focusing on warmth his chest, the fast beat of his heart. Sabrina wondering to herself if the fast beat of his heart was for her or meeting his parents the selfish part of her wanted that beat to be for her, but the selfless part of her wanted it to be of his parents so she went with the meeting of his parents was more important than her, but she hoped that somewhere in that heartbeat of his was for her too.

She smiles up at him with her hand still on his chest a now his hand over hers causing them to look deep at each other "It's going to be okay, you know they will be happy to see you," Sabrina said trying to be supportive of him giving him some encouragement from the looks of him he needed it at the moment, then he almost took her breath away when he slid his other hand across her small, waist bring her in tightly to him facing each other like they were the only ones in the room she felt his hard muscled body move, she wanted to get lost in his dark brown eyes that were a dark chocolate one true weakness was chocolate. "You're sure?" he asked needed some assurance from her that things will be okay with his parents once they see each other, since she had been working for his parents for a while trying to get some insight from her would help him a lot, she then leaned in further closing the small space between them given him that most breathtaking smile that lite up her beautiful face "I have no doubt that everything will be just fine, promise."

Then a sudden crash of a dinner plate hitting the floor breaking the spell that was cast on the two would be lovers if time would allow them to be causing everyone including Jack and Sabrina to look at the kitchen.

Julia could believe her eyes when she saw the man that walked toward Sabrina, tears started to form in her green eyes that have aged over the years. Julia had dreamed of this day would finally come true when her baby boy would finally come home, where he belongs she didn't care how he left all those years ago, seemed to disappear into thin air. Now that he was here in the Diner she was going to do all she can to get this family back together hopefully with Sabrina's help Julia wonder if Sabrina knows who that man was standing in front her was, from the looks Jack was giving Sabrina already knows, Julia thought "hmm, I wonder how she knows, but right now Julia want to get to her son first and hug him for all his is worth which was priceless because her baby boy was home..

She gasps dropping the dish in her slippery hands, she quickly took the strings of the apron she had on, quickly taking off the apron putting it on the counter. Julia rushed to the kitchen door pushing it open to get a better look at her grown boy, she is amazed at how much Jack looks like his father from his height to his dark features he was his father's son.

Sabrina looked toward the kitchen door where Julia stood staring at the man that stood before her with a look of disbelief on her face with pure joy like the greatest gift was given to her except when Jack was born, Sabrina was sure of.

Jack stood next to Sabrina looking where she was looking at, his dark eyes began to pool in the depths Sabrina never witness a grown man like Jack cry before, not even her father when she met him for the first time at his hotel when she found out he was here she was almost jealous of the scene in front of her she sees the love Jack has for his mother, she wished she had that with her mother but she didn't.

Julia was staring at Jack wondering if she was

dreaming this then Jack looks back to Sabrina with a small grin on his handsome with tears coming down his cheeks, he whispered back at her "Thank you." sending warm shivers through her loving this kind of moment in life when all is good in the world.

It was like time stood still everyone in the lobby was waiting with bated breath to see what happens next in the scene that is set before them.

"Oh! Jack is that really you!" Julia cried, whipping her hands onto her white apron, placing her hands to her cheek trying to make sure she wasn't dreaming that this was real that her son was here in the diner looking at her with tears in his eyes too.

Jack looks at the tiny, frail-looking woman that is his mother with her curled red with little white strands of hair at the sides being held with little black combs her tiny frame was wrapped in her waitress uniformed that hung loosely on her she lost some weight that bothers him some because wondered with him being away the stress from the way he left would haunt him for the rest of his life wondering if staying would have changed things.

"M-mother!" Jack softly gushed with a large smile on his face.

He felt his tears began to run down his cheeks, then all the guilt began to wash away from him, when he rushed towards his mother, she towards him, throwing her tiny arms around his neck squeezing him for all he is worth, making everything that happened in the past vanish into thin air. Jack genteelly lifted his mother being careful not to crush her with his full strength.

Then both mother and son began to cry uncontrollably, hugging and kissing the cheeks of each other not wanting this moment to end as if mother and son were the only ones in the room nothing else matters Julia looks up to heaven to say a silent prayer to the big man upstairs for finally answering her long overdue prayers.

How Julia would pray every night for this moment that Jack was alive, well and safe, he would finally come home, her husband and son would finally mend their differences, even if it means that she would have to lock the two stubborn men of hers in a room, by themselves so she could have her family back together again, but Julia knows in her heart that she didn't have to go that extreme she knows that in her heart and soul that Al missed Jack just as much as she did. Julia cheerfully said to Jack "and your father will be so happy to see you!" like freezing time as if nothing else matters but for them.

Jack felt the heavy weight of guilt he felt all those years ago begin to lift off his shoulders, but the doubt was there still until he saw his father face to face, he wanted to believe his mother, she never stirred him wrong before, at that moment everything was okay or will be for him and his old man.

Jack as yet to see his father judge what his reaction might the nerves he felt before meeting his mother was coming back to him.

Jack hope his mother speaks the truth, his mother

has never lied to him before, in the paste, but trust has lead him to women that have screwed, one works for his folks, not Sabrina thou and he has yet to see her, right now meeting his folks was more important, but facing his ex-was one meeting that he wished that he didn't have to face at all, Jack will face her too Midnight wasn't big.

It was hard for Jack to trust anyone especially with Brenda cheating on him before his graduation with one of his best friends, then the fight with his old man, and what he has been through with his music, has not been easy, Jack just needed to see his father face first to make things okay, what his father reaction will be Jack didn't know.

"Oh! Jack, I can't believe that you're here standing in front of me." Julia, cheerfully she then places her tiny hand on Jack's cheek to make sure he was real and not a dream.

Then Jack picks up his mother gently being careful not to crush her with his embrace. "You're not dreaming mom, it's really me?" Jack trying to control his emotions while still holding his mother in his arms, they pull back from each other trying to get a better look at each other "Oh! I have missed you so much!" Julia cried, "Me too! Mom!" Jack cried "Me too!"

"What are you doing here?" Julia gushed happily trying to control her emotions, but her excitement could not be contained and with a little confusion she looked up lovely at her baby boy. "Well, I was thinking, hoping to move back here to Midnight."

"Maybe hopefully open up a recorded company here, have an office for my fan club, if that's okay with you and of course dad." Jack asked his mother for permission to finally come home, like he was a little boy again. "Okay, are you kidding me that more than okay that's perfect!" Julia said cheerfully but taking a back that he would ask such a question. "You're a father is going to be so happy to see you!"

"You really think he will be happy to see me after all this time?" Jack asks sounding doubtful, but hopeful at the same time. "Oh! I'm quite sure he will be "Julia said sounding all confident then she looked around her.

Feeling all eyes on them Julia quickly turned toward the lobby full of people introducing her son to everyone that was there. "Everyone, I want you all to meet my boy, Jack. Who has finally come home for good this time except for when he has to tour, he is the lead singer of the famous rock group 'The Texas Tornadoes'" Julia proudly. Jack looked down at his shoes feeling a little embarrassed over the fuss that his mom was making over him like he was a little boy after he made a home run or something.

Then Jack looks up at the other beautiful woman in the lobby other then his mother he almost forgot was there with tears in her eyes wonder if those tears were for him or something else he didn't know, but they did look like these were happy tears for him it seemed for his mother as well too because he could sense that was a closeness between them which would make being with Sabrina a lot easier on him if his mother like the woman that he was with.

Jack just smiled and nodded at the crowd that just shouted: "Hi and WELCOME HOME!" Jack turned back toward his mother asking her "Mmm, where is Pop?" looking around the lobby, through the serving window trying to locate his old man, getting butterflies in the pit of his stomach again with his nerves wanting to get the meeting with his dad over with, dreading it at the sometime.

"Oh! He is in his office you know business doesn't stop no matter what right!?" Julia said cheerfully she takes Jack by the elbow "Come, let us go and surprise him, okay!" Julia said happily "He is going to be so happy to see you."

Has she gently squeezes Jack's elbow stirring them through the swinging door as they walk toward the office, Jack slowly pushes open the door allowing his mom to go first.

Sabrina just watched the family reunion that took place in front her, then she looks at the family picture that was hanging above the serving window, looking at the younger version of Jack Taylor, then she looks at his broad shoulders then she slowly glanced down his back her blue eyes resting on his tight ass that barely fit loosely in his faded blue jeans. Sabrina continues to watch him as he helps his mother through the kitchen door.

When Sabrina notices that he was looking at her giving a look that almost took her breath away, all she could do is smile at him then he winked at her causing Sabrina to blush a little as she continued to watch him with his mother "Well, there goes my boring summer and love life." Sabrina said quietly to herself of the excitement that Jack might be adding to Midnight and to her life.

"Okay, Randy, I want two rolling racks of half a dozen hamburger buns," Al said on the phone "and let see…"

A soft "Tap!" on the door came through startling Al causing him to jumped little he gets so caught up in his work, in frustration Al shouted at the door "to come in!" while still talking on the phone with, Randy, his bread man trying to finish up his order for next week before the day is through.

Al glaring at the door waiting for the person to show his or her face ready to curse at them for scaring him for one then interrupting him while he conducting business in his office: ordering, pay the bills, part of running the diner, he didn't like being interrupted his wife knows this, when he sees her red, curly head popped out from the small opening of the door with a happy, goofy grin on her pretty face causing Al to grin a little making being mad at her a little hard.

Julia waltzed into the office with a little happy dance, but what Al' saw wasn't seen in a while which was mostly tears that circled her green eyes, a look that Al had not seen in a long time since the night he asked her to be his wife, or since Julia and him were teens, with a little annoyances his voice "hold on Randy, MY WIFE has something important to say to me at least she better." Al snapped looking at his wife as she continued to stand in front of his desk with a little happy step like she was dancing for him or something.

Julia could hardly control herself, she looked lovingly at her handsome husband of 35 years she has been waiting for this moment for a long time with her husband and son meeting face to face, since that stormy night 12 years ago, to become that close family again she could hardly stand it.

Julia had prayed long and hard for this moment "Oh it is, or should I say HE is!" Julia said cheerfully robbing her hands together with a little glee in her eyes as she moved closer to the office door Julia open up the door wide and announced: "I have someone that I want you to meet."

A tall figure of a man appeared in the opening of the door Al just stared at the man that stood in the doorway of his office. Al could not believe his eyes he had to blink twice to make sure that he was not looking at a ghost of his teenage son, but instead of a teenage boy there stood in front of him was a tall man that was a spitting image of him, when he was a young man when Al was Jack's age.., tears began to fill his eyes when he remembered the last time the two spoke to each other or fought all those years ago.

Then the disembodied voice of his bread man came over the receiver of the telephone reminding Al that he was still on the phone, trying not to choke on his word his emotions were on overdrive with seeing his son right now.

Al told Randy on the phone "Hum, Randy someone just walked into the office. I will call you back in a few minutes. Okay, Bye!" Al just barely spoke managed to put the receiver on the cradle.

Jack smiled at his old man trying hard to control his nerves while he watched his father as he rolled back his chair got up slowly to stand next to his desk. Jack was taken back with his dad's appearance how old and haggard he looked wearing a peach, yellow golf shirt, brown polyester pants, and penny loafers.

Jack had hoped to 'God' that he wasn't responsible for his dad's aging, but somehow in his soul Jack knew that he was partly responsible, which made this meeting with his old man much more difficult along with his mother's aging too, will be hard for him to deal with as time goes by, but he had to find the way to make things right with his parents especially his dad. "Hi, ya! Pop!" Jack managed to say in a very nervous voice but trying to keep a smile on his face while trying to control the emotions that were desperate to overtake him.

Al leaned against the side of his desk while looking at his son amazed over how big and tall Jack has gotten over the years those years have been kind to Jack, he looks healthy a little age around his eyes. What Jack didn't know was that Al has been following Jack with his career through the years watching interviews, listening to his music and even went to a concert when Jack performed in Oklahoma City.

Al allows his mind to drift back to that night when he snuck into the show to watch without Jack knowing he was taken aback after witnessing at firsthand how Jack was born to be a performer nothing else Al thought proudly. Al couldn't help, but think about that night how everything changed for them when Jack hit him in the face, stormed out into the night without looking back Al's wasn't so full of pride he would have done the same thing his son did, but his Indian pride and his control over his family especially Jack's life wouldn't let him, he wanted his son do what he did, school and take over the diner so he could retired he wanted the picture perfect family that he didn't realized that he was stumping on his son's dreams no matter if Jack loved music or not, Jack was old enough to know what he wanted Al was just like Jack in a way that he knew what he wanted and no one was going to persuade him from what he wanted to do, but Al's quick temper came between them destroying they're, close father and son relationship.

That night started off well with Jack getting his high school diploma then Al asked Jack what his plans after high school Al were wasn't shocked that Jack wanted music, he knew what was best he knew Jack loved making music he was good at, with him practicing night and day. The screams the cheers especially from the lovely women that wanted him, but Al didn't think that was a good enough reason for building a career in music he was hoping that Jack would go to school and take over the diner s but Al wasn't ready for Jack to tell him he had a different future in mind for him, it wasn't Al's dream which made things between Jack and Al worse but instead of encouraging him to follow his dreams like Jack's grandfather did to Al.

Al remembered that night clearly how furious he was with Jack how dare Jack screw with what Al wanted for Jack. Al remembered standing up getting into Jack's face telling him what a fool he was jabbing his finger into Jack's chest screaming at Jack.

As Al looks back on that horrible night changing everything for them, the angry words that Al wished he could take back "You're crazy, you're fucking crazy, you're not skipping school I saved money for you, now music I thought it was a hobby. Are you NUTS?" Al mocked his hot Indian blood racing through his veins getting hotter as time went on "You won't get anywhere with that kind of career" Al snapped quickly got off the couch getting in the face of his son who had the same temper as Al did. "But dad! Music is my life, you know it!" Jack shouted back "Why do you think I have been playing the past two summers for working my butt off for, my music" Jack snapped, "I thought it was just a hobby you would eventually get over it and settle down!" Al's always wanted to be there for his boy gave him the support that his own dad gave him, but instead he turned his back on his only son if he could take back what happened he would, now here was his chance to make things right he wasn't going to let his son disappear into the night like he did before.

Al blinked bringing him back to the present he looked at his son" hi!" Jack smiled watch his old man he hadn't seen in so long that Jack could tell that time has taken its toll on his father's face and body, with some lines, wrinkles have shown around Al's face along with age spots on Al's hands just like Jack's grandfather had, a long those blood spots whenever he gets injured. Al had let his ounce flat stomach stretch over his black belt; Jack could also see the touch of silver lined his temples on his sideburns along with some thinning of his coal black hair. Al wore matching brown stretch dress slack with dark brown penny loafers along with beach flowered polyester short sleeves, button-down with collar making him look much older than Jack would have liked his dad to be, worried that he might have been the cause of the aging.

"Hi, Ya Pop!" Jack managed to say, letting out the air that he held in his lungs. Al walked a few inches away from his desk to face his son after Jack had stormed out of the house that dark miserable night which was June 6th 12 years ago was edged into his memory like it was yesterday.

Al looks back again he truly didn't mean to let his pride his temper get the best of him when Jack told him that he did not want to go to college Jack wanted a career in music instead of giving Jack the love, the support Al should have given to his son. Al regretted that whole night he wants to go after Jack, fix thing with his, but his foolish Indian pride won't let him.

"You're crazy, Your F—king crazy, you won't get any with that!" Al shouted thinking back on that horrible night. Before Al could blink Jack gave him a one powerful right hook, hitting Al right on the cheek, cutting his lower lip knocking him to the floor, then feeling the sting from the cut on his lip with his tongue, tasting the metal from his blood then touch the twinkling of bleed that started to run down the side of his lip coming from the cut with his fingertips. Julia had knelt beside Al crying with both hands-on Al's shoulder trying to control the situation between her husband and son.

While Al was still sprawled out on the living room floor of their two-bedroom house on Beach wood Street. Al looked up at his son with such anger in his eyes, he shouted out at him with such force Al was afraid that it would have a wake the neighbors.

"You son of a bitch, you get your ass out of this house I don't ever want to see your face ever again as long as I live, do you hear me!" shaking his fists at Jack while he stumbles to his feet. He watched as Jack grabbed his leather jacket gear in hand, with tears in his eyes "I am sorry "with a whisper ashamed to his face, without looking back Jack slams the living room door. Jack rushed to his motorcycle into the downpour of the storm that was brewing outside along with the storm that was brewing inside him right now.

Al shrank into his wife's warm arms crying uncontrollably with his hand covering his eyes while still on the floor not believing what had just happened in a blink of an eye so afraid that Jack would take heed to his words and never come home.

"Hi, son!" Al finally said trying hard not to choke on his words letting his emotions run away from him like that night when things changed for them. Al wanted to fix things with his only child, but his Indian pride won't allow him to take that first steps, his guilt, over that night would not allow him to forget the needed to be solved before time runs out for both father and son, especially when his son was brave enough to come home to face him.

Al looked directly into Jack's dark eyes that were his as well. Al could not hold back what he was feeling, his chin began to quiver, he felt the tears coming from his eyes, then suddenly overwhelmed with emotions he grabbed Jack's shoulders giving him the biggest bear hug. "I am so sorry, I am so sorry," Al, cried, "Please forgive me I never meant what I said that night"!

When Jack heard the forgiveness come out of his father's mouth, Jack began to cry too. "It's okay, Pop, I am sorry too" Jack asks, "please, please forgive me I didn't mean to hit you" has he continue to hold his old man with all his strength. "I know you didn't mean to hit me, son, but the fight started with me not supporting your career choice, I broke the promise I made you when you were a young boy that I would never stop supporting your future choices no matter what they were, please forgive me" Al continues to cry in his son's arms, with a soft sigh and relief rush over them both "All is forgiven. Pop!" Jack.

Then father and son pulled back from each other to get a better look at each other before speaking again, Al places his hands on the side of Jack's face studying the features that were so much like him it not even funny.

"Why are you here?" Al asks with tears still in his eyes as he whips his nose on his ratty old handkerchief. Then Al looked up at his son then smiled for the longest moment still not believing his son was standing there in front of him.

"Well," Jack said has his glances at the floor for a moment, then looks around the office then smiles to himself, how much time had passed but nothing had changed with the décor of the Diner from the lobby to the office. Al was never much into the computer age but has kept upon the repairs to the diner with his old-fashioned filing system.

Jack sees the seven-foot shelving that housed, the canned goods like the peaches, the pears, the chocolate pudding, the ketchup, the bread. Jack sees his dad's fishing rod and net still hanging on the wall behind the door by the shelving on his left side that lined the wall just past the door. Then beside the doorway that lined the wall was the ratty old orange-flowered, but comfy couch that his parents got at a yard sale years ago that once was in the living room of his house.

Then passed the couch was the high school lockers that the employees would keep their personal stuff in then after the lockers are the licenses, awards that Jack had received when Jack was younger the fishing the trips, they took seemed a lifetime ago that hung on the wall. Jack's dad also had his high school, his dad's Jr. College diplomas framed along with the first dollar bill that the diner earned on the wall.

Then facing Jack and his dad on the far wall was the tack board the light gunmetal gray filing, five draw cabinet then the back door that leads to the outside of the diner the wooden and cast-iron park bench where the employees can have their breaks were there.

In the center of the office was his father's five-drawer dark oak desk with a dark brown leather back chair with wheels that Jack's dad and he picked out at an estate sale before Jack left.

"I wanted to hopefully make a permitted stay here except when I tour, which I am in the middle of right now. I should be done in August which would be enough time for Jack to find, open a recording studio, an office and may be a fan club, but mostly I wanted to come home to make things right between you and me, Pop." Jack asked with a touch of sadness in his voice, looking at his hands and then back at his father.

"If that's, okay with you, dad?" Jack asked. Al smiled proudly and said "Well, I am happy you are back.", sounding as though those 12 years never happened Jack was away for work. "You and I do need to talk some more to get things back on track, again, but right now I need to get this order out before next week or I won't have anything to serve, okay?"

Al asked he puts his arm around Jack's shoulders guiding him toward the door leading back toward the kitchen as they stood just outside the doorway of the office "Go, have your mother fix you something to eat you must be starving from your long journey here, alright!" Al asked,

"Okay, thanks Pops!" Jack said as he grinned at his old man, feeling the whole world weight lifted off from his broad shoulders with how well his meeting with his father went now wished he had done it sooner.

"Why don't you come over to the house have supper with your mother and I, around say seven or eight o'clock tonight?" Al ask has he looks at his son with such pride, when he allows his pride to come in between they're tight bond, he won't be standing there in the kitchen of his Diner talking like that fight never happened Al vowed that he would go a long while to allow his foolish pride take control again, what Jack didn't know he supports his career, but silently Al had been following Jack's career from the moment Jack started playing his music in the garage, are a couple of scrape books that housed the newspaper and magazine clippings of many of Jack's accomplishments over the years. Al even attended a concert or two with tickets stubs that he had saved when Al was supposed to be on a fishing trip, someday Al hoped to share these books with Jack to show or tell him how proud of him he was.

"Do you have a place to stay while you are here?" Al asks, "yes, I do it is the beach house that looks out toward the gulf. I would like to show you and mom it soon, but that can wait!" Jack said, "That's great son," Al asked, "We can come over sometime next week to see this rock star palace." "Alright, that will be good," Jack said with a smile, "I think that will be great."

Just then aloud "Growl"could be heard.

Jack looked down at his stomach, then looked back at his old man then chuckled a little "I guess I am hungrier than I thought I better get something to eat." "I guess so!" Al laughs to his son "I'll talk to you later." Jack said cheerfully as he heads towards the kitchen door trying to locate his mother who seems to have disappeared. "I will see and talk to you later Son, okay." Al yelled back at his son causing Jack to turn to face his father "Goodbye, Pop!" Jack said clearly making sure his dad heard him "Bye, son!" Al said. They stood there for a moment looking at each other, feeling happier than before.

CHAPTER 11

Jack scanned the kitchen another moment looking for his mother, not seeing her in this area then he headed toward the kitchen door.

When the door swings back smacking him in the face, causing a sharp pain shooting through his head making him groan in pain. Jack placed his hand on his temple where he was hit. Jack slowly opened his eyes to see which fool hit him with the door as an angelic face of Sabrina he talked to earlier he sighed a little cooling down the temper that was rising.

Sabrina looked around the door to see whom she hit with the door she cringed when she saw who her victim was. The last person she had except to behind the door the last person she wanted to cause pain to be was Jack. "Oh, my God I am so sorry," Sabrina, asked, "Are you all, right?" I didn't see you."

"No, I am fine!" Jack snapped while still touching his right throbbing temple "Who says that a door isn't considered a deadly weapon." Jack jokingly trying to lighten the mood when he saw the look of regret and concern on her lovely face, He could tell she didn't mean to hit him.

Sabrina grabs Jack by the arm, leading him quickly towards her station at the corner of the counter then causing him to sit in the chair as she looks through the drawers for the ice pack. "I will get you some ice, I am so sorry!" Sabrina said, feeling miserable for causing the hurt she had just caused, busing herself looking for the ice pack in the drawer. "Oh! Just great that the most beautiful man, I have ever meet I have to show him my clumsy side after he saved me from being attacked by Steven." Sabrina thought to herself "Hey Darlin it's okay, don't worry about it." Jack said looked around the lobby trying to locate his mother, she doesn't seem to be around.

"Hey sweetheart, do you know where my mom went to?" Jack asked politely "Oh! Your mom went to the store to get some groceries for supper tonight then she said that she was heading home to clean up for your arrival." Sabrina said, looking over her shoulders at Jack with sweet a beautiful smile.

"Did your meeting with your dad go Okay?" Sabrina said as she turns toward Jack with the ice pack in her hand she walks toward Jack, then reaches over the counter, placing the ice pack on Jack's temple causing small pain from the bruise that formed "There that should help you a little." Sabrina said softly trying to be as gentle as possible "Maybe you should go see a doctor?" "No, I am fine, but thanks anyway." Jack answered with a smile as he felt her soft skin from her touch warming the very core of him "the meeting went better then I hoped, thank you." Jack looked at his fingers shyly then looked back at the deep blue eyes that reminded Jack of Saphire jewels wandering to himself why he has never seen this Angel before coming here he wondered how it will be if he touches her like many of her lovers before him would he suffer in comparison.

Then a loose strain of pale blonde hair fell from her ponytail covering her pretty blue eyes Jack gently swept the golden strain carefully placing the strand behind her tiny ear, then softly caressed her cheek amazed at the softness of her skin wanting to touch more of her. When Jack gazed at her small yet very inviting lips wanting but resisted the temptation to taste them this time.

Jack genteelly pulled her face closer to him just breathes away from kissing her, Jack's hungry stomach demand to be heard making its presence known causing them to pull apart from each other quickly glancing at Jack's stomach where the growling sound came from "Well, someone must be hungry." Sabrina said cheerfully thankful for the distraction, trying to make sense of the almost kiss that didn't happen. "Hum, I guess I am." Jack agrees with her, but hungrier for her instead of food.

Then looked away quickly from her trying to figure

out what was happening to him with this woman that he barely met a few days ago "What is wrong with me? I don't even know her yet, I don't know if she likes my music, I should cool things with her." Jack thought to himself angrily.

Sabrina placed her hand into his hand amazed at the size she felt the warmth of his skin as they touched. Sabrina felt warm all over, almost forgetting herself she quickly took a pad from her apron and a pencil from her left ear to write down his order.

"Hmm, what I can get you to eat?" Sabrina asked, looking at him smiles to herself when she sees the dreamy look on his face, she could almost see a little boy in his handsome face wondering what it would be like if she ran her fingers throw his long dark hair forgetting what she was doing.

When she was getting ready to write down his request with a pen and pad in hand. She looks at him and smiled to herself "He is so cute!" Jack leans on his fist said, "I want a hamburger with American cheese, with some hot fries maybe a slice of that cherry pie over there for later!" Sabrina smiles, shakes her head then ask,"Let me guess you want that hamburger loaded, right!" Jack gave her the most beautiful smile then pointed at her then said, "You got it" Sabrina turns towards to the kitchen door walks, still looking at her menu pad, she pushes the door opened to allow herself through it, she stops just past the swinging door. Sabrina puts her hand on her head trying to make sense. How can she be so attracted to Jack so quickly she barely meet him sharing kisses on the beach, in his amazing beach house? She prayed that he didn't feel her racing heart through the touch of her hand with nerves racing through her.

Then, Jared's face appeared in her mind, she quickly vanished his image out of her head. causing her to shake a little. "What the hell," she thought, "why, am I thinking about him, I haven't seen him in years. I hope I never see him again; he is out there looking for her." She thought to send shivers down her back.

Then Jack's voice comes through the other side of the wall bringing her back to why she was in the kitchen for. "Hey, are you okay, I am starving here!" Jack shouted. Sabrina peeked through the serving window with a smile answered, "Oh, I am fine; I was just going over what I wrote down for you. My handwriting can be so messy sometimes, see!" she lied showing him her ordering pad.

She hurries towards the grill and begins to prepare Jack's food. She wipes the sweat from her brow with the back of her hand from the heat of the day as the grill comes alive with the grease of the patty Sabrina placed on it. "Yep, this summer won't be the same!" as she looks at Jack through the window while he reads the Daily newspaper catching up on with what's been happening in Midnight and the rest of the world.

Moments later, she brings out the plate with the hamburger and large mountain of hot fries just the way Jack requested, before she had the chance to put the plate in front of Jack grabs for the hamburger then starts chomping on it then with the other hand, he grabs for a fry he shoves it in his mouth also.

Sabrina watches with amazement over the sight in front of her then asks the stupid question "hmmm, hungry! Then he looked up said "Mm!" nodding his head in an agreement with some hamburger still stuff in his cheek looking more like a boy, then a very sexy rock god that he was he was so adorable to her.

Sabrina shakes her head as she walks back toward the kitchen heading this time for the kitchen sink getting ready to wash some dishes knowing when not to disrupt a hungry man while he is eating.

Sabrina begins to busy herself with the dishes that seem to pile up during the lunch rush, but not hearing him come through the kitchen, but she feels Jack's warmth as he circles his arms around her then places a soft kiss on her temple, it touched her a little that this tough guy can be so sweet towards her without really knowing her.

Jack places his empty dish and glass next to the other dirty dishes, and with a smile on her face Sabrina looks up at Jack and says, "Thank you!" "You're welcome!" Jack answered her. He places a soft kiss on her cheek this time instead of her lips. She wanted this man.

Jack moves on the other side of Sabrina began to help rinse the dishes with her. Sabrina looks up and asks, "How was the meal?" "Excellent, my compliments to the chief the hamburger hit the spot," Jack replied as he places a kiss on her forehead treating her like a long-lost friend instead of a lover. "Why, thank you, sir!"

Sabrina answered in soft drawl "I am so glad to see that my cooking passes your approval, how is the lump?" she asked pointing at his forehead. "Mum, better," Jack replied "You're a cook, a nurse is there nothing else you can do" teasing her a little. "No! I am afraid that's where my talents lie," she answered as she sighs a little.

Jack looks at Sabrina from head to toe then his eyes rested on the curve of her small, but round ass trying hard not to reach down to squeeze. He thought to him "I bet you have more talent than you know of". Then he looked back at Sabrina's face hoping she didn't read him when he looked at her tight ass.

Then he felt the part of his body that was cold for years now grow warm causing his loose jeans to get tighter and his cock harder, he wanted or needed to take things slow with Sabrina he never felt this strong with anyone, not even with his ex-lovers or groupies they never affected him like Sabrina has he didn't realize how uncomfortable his jeans were coming until that moment.

He quickly drew his attention back to the dishes, forcing that part of the body to remain quiet until he can do something about it hoping it would be with, Sabrina, he wanted to do things different with Sabrina treat like she was the most beautiful lady that she is and not some whore.

CHAPTER 12

Brenda watched the two from the doorway of the kitchen, she couldn't believe her eyes when she saw Jack. She had rushed over to the diner after the conversation she just had with Jack's mother when she saw her coming out of the grocery store.

Brenda couldn't believe that Jack had achieved everything he ever wanted and was more famous and very rich too. Brenda could not wait to get her hands on his fame and money only if she could make him forget how she treated him before he left town, but now she has another problem "that little Bitch, Sabrina!" as she glares at the back of the woman's head standing next to Jack laughing, acting like their old friends or something more. "Well!" Brenda fumed silently to herself, "I will take care of this situation once and for all!" "Oh! Jack, darling you're back it's so good to see you, darling!" causing the two at the sink to stop, what they were doing to turn and look at her.

Brenda purred as she sashays towards, Jack, then giving him her most beautiful smile ever then wraps her arms around his neck bringing his lips onto hers thrusting her tongue into his mouth trying to steal his breath like she had done so many years ago. When they were younger, she would use his feelings for her to make older and wealthier boyfriends jealous, but now she wanted Jack and be set for life. Brenda always got what she wanted little twits like Sabrina won't stand in her way, period! She smiled to herself at the embarrassing look on Sabrina's face was priceless, that right bitch! He is mine!" she silently cursed the woman behind Jack's back.

Then Jack quickly grabbed Brenda by the shoulders pushing her away from him causing a little pain towards her shoulders then wiping the lip print on his mouth with his fingers then looking at Brenda with disgust at himself for allowing this to happen. Jack was seething inside with anger for allowing this bitch to kiss him there in front Sabrina, but he was angrier with himself for allowing Sabrina to think that Brenda are lovers and after the way she treated him before he left Midnight, they were over.

What made the situation worse was seeing the look of confusion and hurt in Sabrina's beautiful blue eyes before she left the kitchen leaving the two former lovers alone. Jack forced his attention back to the woman he thought the sun, moon and the stars rose set on when he was a naive little boy that knew nothing of the ways some women like Brenda used their bodies to get what they wanted, until he found out she didn't really care for him like he did for her, she was only using him to get another boyfriend of hers jealous, it killed any trust he had for women. Jack felt his insides go cold inside when he saw the satisfied look on her face when she saw Sabrina leave the kitchen in a hurry.

Then Brenda looks up at him and begins to bat her long lashes at him with an innocent look on her face with a pout "What?" She purred, she began to caress the front of his leather jacket trying to seduce him, making him think she was different, that she cared about him and make him forget the things she did in the past. "Oh, that she will get over it just had to show her that you're mine, I mean it" she purred. Jack had his hands still on her shoulders then squeezed them a little hard making her squeak in pain wishing his hands were around her neck instead squeezing the life out of her.

Jack quickly moved his hands off her shoulders then said gritting his teeth "I want to make this perfectly clear to you stay, the HELL away from me, stay the hell out of my life!" With that he turned stalked toward the door shoving the kitchen door away from him without looking back but looking for Sabrina and leaving Brenda with her mouth wide open in shock!

Brenda places her hand on her forehead in confusion "Am I losing my touch!" she thought to herself still thinking that Jack was this weak, loser that she believes worshiped the very ground she walks on, that she would use to her advantage on countless times. Now Jack hated her, even loathed her, which never happened before in her life. In frustration she went after Jack to make him explain his behavior no one treats Brenda Blair like some white trash, and get away with it, she stops just outside of the kitchen door. To her surprise she sees Jack standing next to Sabrina again trying to explain to her what she saw meant nothing to him, that Brenda and he were over with for a long time, and they will remain that way.

Brenda never thought for a million years that she would have to fight Sabrina over a guy, which she never had to do before this was all new to her. "Jack!" Brenda steamed with her hands on her hips "What does that little, Bitch, have that I don't?" she demanded.

Jack was feeling trapped with Brenda looking at him like he just punched her in the gut, with a bewildered look on her face. Brenda wants to know why he was treating her like dirt on his shoes no one treats her like that and gets away that.

Jack, without thinking, wanting to get away from the situation grabs Sabrina by the hand not giving her a choice to object him.

"Twist of faith" of faith" could be heard of in the distance.

Jack and Sabrina hurried to his bike outside, he turns towards Sabrina "Would you like to go for a ride with me, I haven't been home in a long time; I want to see if this town has changed any!" Jack asks almost pleading with her, feeling his desperation wanting to flee from Brenda's harsh stare that she and Jack was feeling like trapped animals wanting to be free "Okay, why not!" she replied "Let's go, it will be fun." has she glared back at Brenda who was still standing by the diner door waiting for answer that was never going to come.

"JACK! I am waiting!" Brenda fumed. Jack looked over at Brenda then back at Sabrina still holding out his hand toward her "let's go" Jack asked pleading and giving her his warmest smile.

Then Brenda screamed at the top of her lunges stomps back toward the kitchen looking back toward the parking lot where Jack and Sabrina stood. "You, little BITCH, I will get even with you just you wait!" She declared, staring at, Sabrina, through the serving window. "No one steals my boyfriend and gets away with it!" she shouted, "You hear me, BITCH!"

CHAPTER 13

Jack climbs onto his bike first then looks up at Sabrina standing beside him as they looked at each other that felt like forever.

"God, she is so beautiful!" He thought to himself as he watched her in awe as she begins losing her hair from the ponytail allowing it to fall down her back free from the rubber band. Jack fought the urge to reach up to feel the silkiness of the strains that were just loosened.

Sabrina slowly raises her eyes to look at Jack when she feels his dark eyes on her, feeling the warmth that she felt from them. While she undid her hair, feeling a little uneasy from the way he was looking at her. She stops mid-way undoing her hair to ask, "Is there something wrong?" She looked at herself to see if she missed something?

"No!" Jack replied, shaking his head feeling embarrassed, "You're perfect!" watching her look shyly toward the ground with a little blush rising from her cheeks, making her more beautiful to him.

Then they both looked at each other quickly changing the moment he pats the back seat asking her "Are you ready? "Sabrina this time she didn't hesitate to climb on the back of the bike with him. He told her "Come!" has he reaches out a hand to her to help onto the bike, she realize what direction her mind went looking at his large hand wonder what it would feel like on her body the pleasure that would come with those long fingers playing her like a guitar, but what shock her the most was that she allowed it to happen again when she allowed him to kiss her so quickly after she was attacked the night before, Jack as made her feel safe, she couldn't allow her guard down again, with thoughts of her ex still alive and larking.

Then she looked up to see the concern look on Jack's face making her blush again she a little nervous she prayed that he doesn't have the ability to read her mind where her thoughts went when she looked at his hand. He asks her "Are you okay?"

"Yes, I am fine, thank you, but I am not perfect" she replied then took his hand carefully sliding behind him felt her body heat rise a little when she pressed her body against his hard muscled body that making her mind right now. Sabrina hopes to God that he doesn't feel the beat of her heart through the touch of her hand. She then wraps her arms around his waist hugging him a little tight, sensing her nervousness he genteelly caresses her wrist causing her to jump a little. He gently told her "Don't worry, you will be alright, I will keep you safe, I promise!" trying to reassure her that she will be safe with him then he felt her body relax a little. She was deeply touched by his concern for her well-being she did know why she was being so weird around him, she already road his bike once when she just met maybe it was the excitement she was facing with Jack she didn't what was ahead for her, but she is ready for it.

"What is wrong with me I am acting like a girl in heat I need to slow this thing down. I agreed! to go with him, so get over with it!" she chides herself then she smiled to herself because Sabrina could not believe her luck, right now she on the back of his bike that belonging to this incredibly beautiful man that she ever meet who wanted her, which was truly amazing especially when he could have gone after Brenda which floored her to their fighting over the same guy in what universe allowed that to happened.

Jack turns on the engine, rolls the bike back a little stirring the bike around towards the exit leading to the open highway heading to another place for him, back towards the city.

The warm wind wrestles through her golden hair, Sabrina, never felt so alive and free in her life the rush was amazing being on the back of this amazing man's bike. Jack felt her silence he looks through his mirror at her, asked her "Are you sure, you're, okay?" "Oh! I am fine, thank you, for asking, it's just I never felt so alive and free in my life!" she smiled at him as she shouted. Then she throws her arms around, Jack's shoulders hugging him for all he is worth and laughing.

Jack chuckled looking at her through his side mirror enjoying her happy carefree spirit. Then he gently touched her arm, the softness of her skin he felt himself get hard again. He wondered to himself if this was what love feels like he heard his father say a thousand times that his life started when he met his mother before Jack was born.

Jack wanted something different with Sabrina, then the women he had in the past, he wants to treat her like a lady that she is, but the ache in his cock demanded that he react toward her like she was a whore, he wanted to throw Sabrina on the sand bearing himself deep inside her. He can picture the scene in his mind has he trails hot kisses down her neck as if he was starving for her when soft moans escaped her luscious lips, Jack blinked rush that thought from his mind it was all he could to control his body doing all kinds of stuff to his mind, he had to stop or he might wreck his bike.

CHAPTER 14

Jared walks into the small diner approaches the tall, blonde, but very fake done up in a French twist hairstyle with a body that barely fit the waitress uniform, with her big tits almost popping out wanting to say hi to him normally he would be happy to greet them right now he needed to find the one woman that almost cost him destroyed financial dreams the only thing that mattered to him well maybe he could dabble in some pleasure while he was here as he stares at the beautiful pair of tits to him. "Excuse Miss I wonder if you can help me?" in his drop your panties smooth kind of voice with his All American boy smile that seems to get what he wanted especially with the ladies thou his looks have been altered big thanks to the little bitch who helped take out his right eye that gave him a bit of a scar that stopped at his cheek that could have ended his life, but now he was alive and back wanting a little revenge on the woman who cost him almost everything.

Brenda turned around to face the stranger that walked into the Diner. She was a little startled by the look of the stranger she faced when she turned. He was tall, a little thinned that didn't bother her, it was the black leather patch that covered his right eye along with the ugly scar that ran from his eye to his cheek, other than that the man was kind of lovely to her, he wasn't her type with his sandy blonde hair icy blue eyes that gave her the creeps, but what he had to say to her changed her mind. "I was wondering if you know this woman?" Jared asked as he flipped an old photo of Sabrina to the waitress called Brenda that her name tag read "yes, I know her I work with her, in fact, you just missed her she left with my ex-boyfriend. What do you want with her?" Brenda seemed to be unhappy with Jared's ex too which will make this revenge that he wanted that much easier to achieve.

Jared smiled at Brenda using her to get even with Sabrina, no destroy her Jared thought he liked much better. "Well, my dear she is my wife I have been searching for her high and low for her I missed so much, she ran out on me when I caught her cheating on me, I wanted her back, I was wondering if you could help me find her?"

Brenda was stone silence that little bitch is married she dared to call me a whore when they both got into it with each other, well paybacks are a bitch she will be enjoying the most win back Jack and destroy Sabrina at the same time she was all for it. Brenda smiled her best smile possible at the stranger. "I would love to help you." She purred as she caressed the length of his forearm that was dressed in a green knit sweater and a pinstripe button down shirt the stranger had tucked into his loose jeans and brown penny loafers. "Tell me more about your history with Sabrina I would love to know more about her and you?" Brenda grinned and purred she could wait take her revenge on Sabrina and take what she want and that was Jack and his money, be set for life.

CHAPTER 15

"Are you, okay my dear?" Jack asks loud enough for her to hear through the wind as they continue to ride through the dusk as the day slowly gives into the night, while caressing the back of the velvety soft skin of her hand, her arms were still circled around his waist as he felt her tremble a little showing his concern for her. Sabrina looks at Jack through his side mirror trying to think of a cover-up for her silence she felt herself tremble a little with her nerves and excitement over what might lay ahead of her, wherever he was taking her too, when she saw his handsome face through the mirror the chiseled chin, those lips that she already tasted in his house on the beach she already fantasized about them being on her body more than once those chocolate brown eyes seem to warm her to the soul like the rich hot chocolate, like her favorite morning drink does "I am fine, thank you, just admiring the scenery, just wondering where you are taking me now because it is getting dark out."

Sabrina smiled at him trying hard to figure out why she was scared in one moment, excited in the next then angered to herself, she is in competition with Brenda it seems with the same man no less because they never fought over the same man before. Sabrina's attraction toward Jack was getting stronger by the moment she wondered to herself if this was same as her past was or something different like something real what she feels for him.

Sabrina did not know what to expect from this moment on with Jack, she felt shy around him but determined to get something out of this before life comes crashing in on her she feels it coming.

They were flying through the roads, the scenery started to change as they headed somewhere else something new, an eerie, but something familiar to her, but not the beach house. The sunlight they had guided them through the sharp turns and grooves of the streets were being replaced with mountains and forest on one side on the other side where you can see the beachfront of Midnight disappear into the woods which was confusing Sabrina, and scaring her at the same time like her paste was haunting her again biting her causing her to tighten her arms around Jack's waist that caused him to look at her with concern again.

Sabrina didn't think she would face her fears so

soon with a forest of Midnight she didn't know existed she hasn't told Jack of her fears of dark forest and storms, now he was taking her where she was getting scared by the moment this getting too close to old memories she thought long since faded of her past she never wanted to relive again. Sabrina began to tremble a little not from the cool night air, but from a flashback of a dark stormy night when she was young alone fearing for her life, Jared's disembodied voice yelling at her "Sabrina, you bitch where are you, I am coming for you. You can run, but you can't hide I will find you mark my words!".

Sabrina looked up to see a beautiful large cabin, no matter the size big or small, that night so long ago will haunt her for the rest of her life, this cabin had the old logged feel, with a gray stone chimney, wrapped around decking with a single stairway, the last cabin she was in was smaller less impressive than this one Sabrina stood there trying to make this moment different than the one where she was running from life or her old life.

Jack stands near his bike begin to unpack his backpack then he looks at Sabrina when he sees her standing there just staring at the cabin, a look of freight like she was seeing a ghost that has come alive in front of her, getting concern for her as he walks up beside her placing his hand on the small of her back causing her to jump "Hey are you okay, I thought this was a great place to take you to surprise you with because you said you were from Idaho," then takes a deep breath of the fresh forest air that surrounds them looking at the cabin that he bought with some of the royalties that he receives from his music, but this place was more special to him then the beach he would come to here clear his head write his music even got in touch with his native American side of his soul, he loved this place.

Jack was hoping this place would be special to Sabrina too, from the frightening look on her lovely face is proving to be otherwise, he was wondering if he made a huge mistake by taking her here. Jack looked around them now the darkness was creeping in on them it was too late to leave, but within a blink of an eye Sabrina looks up blinking back the tears forcing one her warmest smile on, as if that dark cloud that hung over her didn't happen, that bothered him a lot, but for now he would let it go until she is ready to talk about it.

Jack didn't want to ruin this new thing he was trying to have with Sabrina sharing everything meant the world to him this woman with the killer curves, the legs that seemed to go on forever he craved to have wrapped around his waist as he takes her deep until she screamed his named as if he was a god to her.

If Jack played his cards right now tonight, he would get lucky, he hoped, from the looks of things he might have to go slower then he wanted. Jack was willing to do that if that is what it takes to have this beautiful angel that has touched him in so many ways that no other woman has before not even his bitch of an ex Brenda who was trying to dig her nasty claws into him now that he is back in town, now that he was famous and has butt load of money her favorite topic besides herself, is the only thing she wants he needed to keep his guard up whenever he is near her.

◆◆◆◆◆

CHAPTER 16

"What do you think" Jack asks cheerfully showing off his pride and joy his third favorite place in the world to him where he could come for peace and quiet, away from the noise of being famous where he can be by himself.

Someday share it with someone special then he turned to look at the woman that stood before him. "When I was younger, I would come here when I needed to clear my head or just get away from life. I would climb onto my bike just head out, and come here to the big woods, well not as tall as the trees in California are or where your from in Newkirk, this cabin was very special to me, I promised myself when I hit the big times with my music I wanted to buy with my money this cabin or the land around it, besides the beach house. I wanted this place to go to so if things went well with my folks and they have I would have my special place this place. I hoped that you like it?" his voice faded when he finally looked at Sabrina, instead of a look of happiness on her lovely face he saw the look of sadness and fear like a dark cloud as engulfing her beautiful face her skin has turn ghost white telling him that bringing Sabrina here was a big mistake. "Hey Love, are you okay tell me please we can leave now before it got too dark?" Jack asked with a worried look on his handsome face as he gently touched her skin with his hand sliding down her arm taking her hands into his, causing a warm shiver rushing through her bringing her back to the present as she recalls that time she was in a cabin much like this one, but that time she was young, stupid, and running for her life in a downpour.

The dark cloud that was in her deep blue eyes vanished into thin air like it never happened, with a very cheerful smile that never reached her eyes, he knows in his soul that was a cover. "I am fine!" she said cheerfully "Are you sure? We can go somewhere else if you want?" as he caressed the side of her cheek causing the warmth of his touch warming her blood she didn't want to ruin this once lifetime moment for her with this very beautiful and sexy man beside she needed to put some old ghosts to rests except the ghost out there that still haunting her until he finally finds her, she just hope when that happens she will survive that encounter when it comes so she can be freed. "No, I am good, seriously!" she said in a nervous giggle, "There is no other place

I want to be than here with you!" trying to be more convincing that she was happy to be there with him.

This time Sabrina with her hand still in his enjoying the warmth that he was providing her, beginning to like the feeling that his touch was giving her, the strength, and the confidence, he didn't know that he was giving to her facing her demons and fears she knew she would have to face before she could totally move on with her life and finally be happy. Sabrina had hoped that Jack would be the one that would be around, when her past finally catches up with her, she knows Jared won't give up until he finds her. The question is will Jack be there for her when the shit hits the fan, Sabrina hoped.

Sabrina comes back to the present standing in front of her is this beautiful, handsome, and sexy man that towers over her his warm hard muscled body that gives most girls dream of could be hers if she plays her cards right.

To change the mood Jack decided to pick her up causing her to squeal a little, putting her over his shoulder, she pounded on his back then he swatted her ass as he marched into the cabin to cheer things up then he gently dropped her onto the couch that was beside the fireplace. Then he pins her hands on each side of her head, Jack placed his lips on her lips looking deep into her eyes wanting to deepen this moment with her in silence, deeping this soft kiss he slides both her arms up pinning them above her head placing both her hands into his powerful left hand, part of her was tensing up because she didn't know him all that well she was getting a little excited about what was happening with this gorgeous, hunk of man who was kissing trying to steal her breath away, warming her to the core making her wanting more from him, he needed to make his point across she thinks he wanted to make out with her on this old comfy couch that seemed to match that rest of the log cabin that has a warm glow coming from the stone brick fireplace he had started before he took there.

Jack slid his right hand up Sabrina's rib cage that she felt through her waitress's uniform until his hand found what it was seeking resting under the lobe of her left breast. Jack gently squeezed her very firmed, but lovely tit, it wasn't big, it wasn't small either, it fits perfectly in his hand, plus it was real much unlike the women he normally with ,half laying on top of her, at the moment, thou part of him wanted to take his time with this amazing woman who seemed to be willing to let him, to have his way with her, his right hand and the rest of his body seems to have a mind of their own as soon as his hand touch her tit still covered in her uniform which wasn't that thin, he could feel the hardness of her tip he was losing all reasoning like his mind went on vacation or something with his hand softly molding, squeezing the perfect tit causing a soft gasp and moans to escape from her sweet lips with a tiny opening of her mouth.

Jack took advantage of the opening of her sweet mouth plunged his tongue cut off any speech or protest that she might have had to change her mind before ending the kiss, he wanted to continue to see where this might lead hopefully with them both naked in bed and on this couch, they were on.

As quickly as the third kissed happened, the second kiss they had shared was hot the first was sweet, almost a test, this kiss was something else it left Sabrina breathless, mindless, crazy for more, she didn't care what happens she wanted no she needed this like she was a starved woman for something sweet and hot Jack was the cook.

"Now my love here are the rules, you are a guest here, that means no lifting a lovely finger with cooking, or cleaning that is my job your job is to enjoy your time here." He said in a deep sexy voice making clear that he was the boss and not her, his house his rules again, being the stubborn woman that she was no one tells her what to do even if this cabin was his, as they continue to lay on the couch he on top of her "Oh really what if I want to make you supper or help clean this wonderful cabin out in the middle of the big woods, that needs a woman's touch?" she asked back, as she with her freed hand caressed his chest that was still covered in a button down Red and white squared flannel shirt, with her finger just stopped above his already enlarged cock that seems to tighten further in his loose jeans making his dick bigger from her empowering teasing he was loving this power play that they were having right now is this what their future to be he hoped.

Jack quickly placed his full mouth on hers silencing her for a moment, leaving her breathless and causing her body to warm all over again making her to wondering with a smile how long her time with him will be while they were there in the cabin he was so proud of, "The answer is no my house my rules." he answer back "man you are bossy aren't you?" she growled back not liking the fact someone she barely knows has the upper hand with her, she did come here of her free will she will do what he wants with-in reason. "What if I break these rules of yours?' she purred back letting him know she wasn't a pushover she won't bend just for anyone unless he gives her a reason to right now, she had to admit it to herself, she wanted to see how far this new relationship goes.

"Well, my dear, I will have to show you the who is boss, by putting you over my knee and paddle your sexy behind," he answered as a matter of fact, with a raised eyebrow at her making sure she heard him

"Sexy?" "Yes, very". "So, you find me sexy, do you?" she asked with a cheeky grin while pinned underneath him on his couch that lined the wall that divided the living room and kitchen with the staircase leading up to the loft. "Every inch!" he answered as he gazed up and down her lovely face, she liked the look on Jack's handsome face "damn how lucky is she." she thought to herself.

To make his point to her about how sexy he thought of her, he quickly placed a hungry kiss her sweet lips again deeping the kissed Jack his large hand from her wrists slid to her rib cage was still wrapped up in her waitress uniform, resting under the round lobe of her other breast. Sabrina let out a soft, muffled gasp causing her to open her sweet lips further Jack took the opportunity with his tongue to caress the inner lining of her sweet mouth, he thought he was on a high the sweetness that Sabrina was providing with her soft mouth.

Jack stopped the make-out session with this wonderful angel he wanted to get to know before he got too deep into her physically, he desperately wanted to, with her long pale blonde hanging loosed free from her tie fanned out over the pillow that laid in the corn of the arm of the couch made her look like an angel with a halo. If he were to searched her bare back when they finally make love would he find her wings that she might be hiding under her tight waitress uniform?

"How about we stopped for a moment so I can give you a tour of this cabin that's like my second home to me or third home." he asks has he got up off of her and the couch where Sabrina was laying there feeling confused, little hurt she wanted more like he was letting her to adrift away from him on the ocean, did he find her desperate or what she didn't know, then he turned around offered his hand to her "come I want to show you around tell you why this place was so special to me" in his smooth voice he went on to explain why he loved this place the quietness the serenity he needed with his life being crazy being a rock god to millions of his adoring fans then she realized he was trying to share his life with her the places that meant a lot to him she was becoming more to him then she thought she wasn't just a fling to him he needed to satisfied an urged he needed to scratch at least that is what he is trying to convey silently to her, at least she hoped she was trying to read in between the lines he wanted more from this, he could tell she too wanted more, not getting the silent message that he was sending to her or her body wasn't. Sabrina will go along with what he wanted for now.

Sabrina will let him know sometime in the future that if he is the one for her she wanted more than the hot kisses he was giving her here and there she needed the physical too, not just the emotional connection she needed from him, not this stopping and going with him isn't helping the situation with her, it was confusing her.

Sabrina won't settle for less, she will play this game with him as he leads her through the cabin showing her the tiny kitchen that was off limits to her as he clearly stated before so was the cleaning which was his job as well he will see that she wasn't going to be a pushover if he wanted to be with her they were going to have to come to an understanding she will be helping with the cleaning and the cooking when it comes to it.

✦✦◆✦✦

CHAPTER 18

The kitchen was very tiny the sink and counter was in the middle with space on each side facing the front window of the cabin on the other side of the stairway with the stove in the corner by the sink and the refrigerator by the door with the cabinets down and above the frig, the stove with the window between the cabinets which was a two story cabin with a pitch roof, everything about the cabin screamed, rustic and simple, nothing about Jack seemed anything, but those things yet they seemed to fit him perfectly, maybe that is why Sabrina is so drawn to him that Jack has this tough as nails kind of image, that everyone sees when they look at him with his black leather jacket and loose jeans, biker boots that most people would fear, there was more to him than meets the eye she sees that in him when he isn't this Rock god/ biker guy in an appearance.

The old refrigerator that was eggshell white that had the metal door handle and hinges and the cabinets were put together by hand she could tell that because simplicity and the ruggedness of the old kitchen that was paint color lime green Sabrina wonder if the color was picked by the man himself or someone who lived their life for the outdoors that they wanted the comfort of home, but the roughness of the outdoors.

Jack asked her "Come I want to show you the rest of this place." he offered her his right hand again she took it gladly as he guided her throughout the small cabin was a skeleton before he found it when he was a younger trying to make his way into this life trying to figure out what he wanted in life and he would add bits and pieces of home saving with little money that he had to fixi it up, then when he left town this was one of the last places that he went just after he stormed off into the dark night from his folks after their fight after he graduated from school. Has he looked back on his life back then about how scared he was he really didn't know what he was going to do or where he wanted to go because every place he wanted to go to was so far away from Midnight, Like L.A., New York, Chicago or even Cleveland? He ended up in first Memphis Jack figured if The King got his start there, he thought why not him, but it was much harder for him to start there then he thought too. He even played different clubs here and there just to get his foot into the doors of the music business.

Has Jack's explained his life with Sabrina she came away thinking that she began to be in awe of this man standing beside her he was sharing his life before her, she was a little jealous of him. Jack knew what wanted he went after it; he also had the love and support of two great people. she never had that with anyone at all the men in her life either told her what they thought she wanted to hear, so he could get what they wanted from her then leave her to want them then when they got what they wanted from her they walked away or they tried to kill her because she found out the truth about them they never wanted her in the first place, only what they can get from her.

Sabrina just continued to look at, Jack, as they stopped at the large King sized bed as they came up from the tall staircase that leads up to the loft that barely fit big king sized bed that had large logs as post that looks like it is held by some thick rope holding it together, but she can see the rope was for show that the blots and screws held it together. It looked comfy to her the mattress was covered white sheets, with red and white squared quit that looked like that it was well used and soft when she touched it he said that he took the quilt with before he left town from his parent's house that night his grandmother made from stripes of fabric that came from his father and grandfather's old shirts he was given to him on his 12th birthday he was so fund of his grandparents his life changed when they passed away killed in a car crash just after his 12th birthday he gets chilled every time he thinks of them wondering if their proud of the man he has become. He sits on the bed as he caresses the quit as he thought about those two special people, how much he has missed them and how happy he was that he came back to see his folks that it was the right move for him then he rested his dark eyes on the lovely lady that was resting on the bed with as he told her the story of his life at this moment. Then he points to the bathroom that has the door closed on the other side of the bed and five drawer dresser all the logs and wood had the golden stain color that seemed to give a soft warm glow that have made the ghosts of Sabrina's past disappear for the at least for the moment until the one that is still alive that is out looking for her that is haunting her every awaking moment, comes to finish what he didn't get to do before she ran away from her old home back in Idaho until that ends for her and if she lives through then she would be able to move on with her new life.

Then she felt Jack's warm hand cover her hand that startled her little bring her back to the present "Darling, are you okay you look pale, are you thinking about the other night with those three fuckers whoever they are going to hurt again I promise?" Jack said with a concern sound in his voice.

CHAPTER 19

S abrina knew in her heart and soul someday she is going to have to tell about her past the how and why she came to Texas in the first place, not for the white sandy beaches, but to escape and hide from Jared her life in Newkirk she had worked so hard to rebuild from the nightmare after her 19th birthday the day when she found out her boyfriend she loved more than life its self and she thought loved her was the devil himself.

She remembers going through that moment in her life like it was scary movie it felt like a nightmare coming true where you are running through the pitch black forest alone without help from anyone with a lightening overhead, a down pour someone who you once loved dearly and trusted out there chasing shouting your name wanting you dead when they finally catch up with you that part of Sabrina's past she knows she needed to tell someone maybe the weight of that heavy burden knowing that she almost killed someone she loved once, after she confronted him with his truth, why he hooked up with her when she was just 19 was barely out of high school. Sabrina was scared that if Jack knew that she almost killed someone else she loved he never look at her in the same way he would not want anything to do with her, she could not bear to lose this good and kind man who saved her.

They seemed to be made for each other by the way they connected from the moment they met they have not let go of each other since.

"Hey where did you go; Sabrina are you okay?" Jack asked with a concerned voice as he caresses her hand, she turned her hand to clasp his hand was so warm to the touch, she wondered what it would be like to have that hand caress the rest of her body has it come alive with that one touch he was giving her.

Sabrina spread a fake smile on her face "I am fine I was just thinking how amazing this place was, I loved the mountains where I am from." "Oh, really where is that?" he asked "Newkirk, Idaho," she answered as she continued to lay the large bed that fills up the whole space of the loft, she loved it was soft and comfy something she never felt before was safe.

What she like most about Jack he made her feel wanted he has only given her hungry kisses some caresses that left her wanting more, she needed no she needed more she was a starving woman it wasn't for food. What, was this thing she was feeling, she was afraid to place a name to call what it was or might be this undeniable attraction that she had for Jack she could sense he felt the same way she felt about him? She didn't know what this thing was between Jack and her, she was willing to see it through if he was willing, she didn't dare ask him in case she was wrong about him.

"Hey, where did you go again?" Jack asked to bring her back to the present maybe she was overthinking things with him she does misread things with people her track recorded can test to that case in point Jared, her trust into people has gotten her into trouble she won't be.

She could be looking at her possible future right now with Jack, the only questioned she had would Jack be there if and when her past comes crashing forward waiting to ruin her future as they lay here on the bed in this almost run down cabin that is similar to one that she was running from in the middle of the night in the rain trying to save her life, but she knows in her heart and soul that Jared isn't done with her.

"I am here, I was just thinking about what this whole thing between us is because I barely know you I feel like I know you my whole life, what are we friends or more than friends?" she asked him hoping that she is reading this situation with Jack right that he wants this as much as she wants this too with his manly beauty takes her breath away as she reaches with her hand, she runs her fingers through his hair he has the most beautiful black hair like the color of coal it was soft like that of a raven's wing, that feathered around his handsome face, she caress the right side of his face loving the warmth of his skin beneath her finger tips as she continues to caress his smooth skin on his chin felt firm she also felt the prickly hairs of a beard started she felt the heat burning through her vanes warming her blood.

she wanted more from him if he didn't give this thing that she so desperately wanted she knew that there was no going back from once they passed this thrust hold if he decided to reject her at this moment she knows she won't try again this was it for her the life she wanted for her future will be gone forever then she will continue to believe that love does not exist to her.

Jack takes the soft hand that was caressing his cheek he wanted to closed his eyes allow the warmth of her touch cherish the feeling she was giving him at the moment even the touch was innocent it was giving him wicked thoughts he wanted to push her down take all of her clothes off of her, the gentleman side of took over first he wanted to see where she wanted to go with this allow her to take the lead.

Jack kissed the inside of her hand has her fingers caressed the bottom of his full beautiful mouth she wanted that mouth on her like now she wasn't going to stop until that mouth was touching her she almost could not breathe the feeling of wanting him was overwhelming her.

Jack and Sabrina continue to lay on the bed they were on waiting for the one to make the first move like they were in a stalemate until Jack played with the tiny button that came together like a 'V' in the middle of her cleavage he began to undo the button but stopped he didn't want to push her in case she wasn't ready for it he would be okay with that he was more than willing to see if she wanted this she showed him that she did wanted more when she reached for the same button with fingers began to undo the buttons she wanted more no she needed more she wasn't going to stop.

Jack took her hands placing them on each side of her beautiful face with her long blonde hair pillowed around her head making her look the angel he thought she was, pressing both her hands on the pillow he climbed on her pressing her further into the mattress.

Sabrina thought she was dreaming or fantasized about this beautiful man who was on top of her, placing soft kisses on her forehead than on the sides of her cheeks her nose causing her to a smile loving the tenderness she felt cherish she didn't want to be cherished like she was a small child which she wasn't she was a grown ass woman that she wanted the heat he was building in her she felt head go light like she was on a drug that any moment she was about to exploide into a million pieces, she was acting like the guy in this and he was the girl taking his own sweet time making love to her face than he placed his face was between her cleavage kissing and licking up her throat causing a soft gasp to escape from her mouth, then capturing her lips with his teeth loving the sweetness the warmth from her mouth, soft moans escaped from each other has the fire began to build growing hotter out of them both.

Jack looking into her beautiful blue eyes that deepened in color when she was in the depth of her desire in the midst of having sex he liked he wanted to be the gentleman here to make sure that she was getting what she wanted. Sabrina reaches his buttons to his flannel shirt quickly undoing the buttons felt there were a million buttons it felt it took forever to open his shirt to get to his chest she placed soft kisses on his skin the chest hair was tickling her nose she placed her hands on the side of his neck.

Jack closed his eyes he felt he was in heaven or flying with this amazing woman who has shown him more passion more than any other woman who was made for him.

Jack didn't know her well but didn't care all he wanted was this moment at this time with this tiny woman was giving him a major head rush from her mouth to her gentle touch causing his whole body especially his large cock to grow hard in his loose jeans were becoming more uncomfortable when she opened his shirt revealing his broad shoulders and chest placing soft kisses on his skin she smelled of roses and honeysuckle her favorite scents was seared into his memory wherever he went from this moment on when he sees a rose or smell a honeysuckle flower he will think of her.

Jack took the rest of the buttons of her pink waitress uniform began to undo them all, placing kisses on her shoulders then on her mouth her smoothed skin was he knew several models who would kill to have her perfect skin it was perfect and warm if heaven had a scent to him it would of honeysuckle and roses he wanted to drown in this scent of hers.

He laid her down further on the mattress he didn't want this moment to end no matter what happened to them both, the world could end and he didn't care he would worry about the world later.

When he and Sabrina have this little cocoon for them even, thou time was short for them but nothing else matters to them except each other.

CHAPTER 20

Jack took the clasp of her simple pure smooth cupped push up with a pink laced inlay that pushed her beautiful tits up for all to see for now his eyes only he wanted to see them this sexy woman's breast his hungry hands wanted to touch, squeezed, mold feel the heaviness of them he couldn't wait to see like it was a gift that kept on giving.

Her tits weren't big, but not small either they fit perfectly into his hands has he gently cupped and teased the rosy tips of her nibbles causing Sabrina to wimbled and moan as she felt him take one of her nipples into his mouth sucking and pulling causing her to breath heavy, as he played with the other tip with his pointing finger and thumb causing the tip to harden, with his continual caresses, kissing and licking causing her to gasp, moaning and arching her back trying to meet his demand she sighed slowly losing the control over her body she welcomed this lose as she moaned Jack's name like it was a prayer urging him on with his focus on her as she hugged his face tight to her breast has he continue his beautiful torture on her body.

Jack gently lays Sabrina back on the bed he takes her hands in his big powerful hands gently places them on both sides of her head, then wiggles his finger at her "no touching!" this is for your pleasure only" as she arch an eyebrow at him that she didn't care for his bossiness at that moment, but didn't want to argue with him in the middle of making her fantasy come true with this beautiful man who is a sex god to millions of women that have come to his shows, if she was a betting woman right now they would all be jealous of her right now especial his ex, Sabrina quickly banished her from her head she didn't want to think about anything else except Jack and him alone.

Sabrina moves her hands to his neck in defience then he places her hands on the side of her face, he tells her "No he was firm this time, he would make sure she was tied to the bed the next time if she moves again he wanted all her pleasure to be focus on her and not on him.

Jack would make sure they both got what they wanted out of this moment that leaving them both satisfied when this moment was done here Jack wanted more with this woman he didn't know what form that may be right now he was opened to anything except for marriage he wasn't ready for that yet neither was she, it was too soon for both they needed to get to know each other first there was a lot that he didn't know about Sabrina he knows she has secrets that kept hunting her especially involving this cabin or cabins periods he knows she wouldn't come here by herself with her actions seeing this place when they arrived they will deal with that later when the time comes to talk about it right now he had more important matters to take care of like making this lovely lady come.

Jack placed soft kisses just below her two breasts then liked his way down her honey trail that leads to the promised land of her beautiful folds the mixture of her personal scent that of honeysuckle and rose was intoxicating to him making him drunk or high it didn't matter to him he was enjoying it.

Sabrina was still this angelic figure minus her wings and right now her clothes Jack took off her with blonde hair look like a halo spread out surrounding her lovely head Jack didn't want to go to hell for this next move at least he will be smiling his way down meeting the devil himself. "What the hell, why not!" Jack spoke out aloud as he places kisses on her thighs causing Sabrina to raise her head to look at him a questioning look arching her eyebrow too, she asked shyly "What?" "Nothing you're so beautiful!" he answered, causing a blush to form on her lovely cheeks "Your weird, I think you need your eyes checked you're seeing things that aren't there," she answered in a soft hush why does her mouth feel so dry trying hard to keep her wits about as she feels him getting closer to the center of her pussy like he was saving the best part of her for last as he blows on her pubic hair torturing her a little, she pleaded with him to end this beautiful slow torture he was giving her with him studing the design of her pussy and continues to blow on her taking his time which was driving her insane right now "Please Jack!" she pleaded with him to end her suffering, but he wasn't done with his torturing he caressed the skin, the hair coming to the edge of her pussy, but not going further prolong her aguney, her pleasure.

Jack didn't like being doubted by anyone especially when he spoke the truth "Please, what?" he asked with a smirk knowing he was killing her slowly with his soft touch and breathe on her pussy then asked that stupid question like he didn't know what she wants but he was stalling his foreplay he was getting a kick out of this when he showed who was the boss in this and it wasn't her.

Jack crawled up her pinning her arms against the pillow placing a hot, but a rough kiss on her mouth sending up red flags changing the hot and heavy atmosphere to a cold and tense one as he covers her mouth with his hand silencing her "First when I say you're beautiful I mean it, don't doubt me, or questioned me, most of all don't mock me, please" he said firmly as he slid down her to continue what he started.

Sabrina was confused now she wasn't so sure she wanted him to continue, but what he just said and did scare her when all this time he made her feel safe, but now no that was when she stopped him which confused him too wondering what he did wrong and how can he make it right he was clueless.

Sabrina quickly got off the bed grabbing her uniform putting it on to cover her nakedness wrapping tightly around her like it was her only protection to face him, she knew that she was overreacting to what he said and did, but she had been through too much hell with men first her father, step-father, Jared and then Steven, now Jack too no she wasn't having it not with him".

Darling what is wrong, please tell me?" he asked almost pleading with her trying to figure out why she got freaked with tears beginning to form in her beautiful blue eyes he didn't want too see those tears when things where going so amazing with them what did he do to screw things up which he never thought he did in this maybe he was misreading this scene with her he didn't know again clueless until she spoke vanishing the tears quickly like they were never there or she didn't want him to see them, when he did.

Sabrina was standing there trying to figure out what to say without revealing her whole life history to this man sitting patiently waiting for her to say something to clue him in why she stopped him. "Jack you have come to mean a great deal to me, you saved my life I owe you. I really want us to work out, but I will spare you the gory details of my past I am not ready to share with you, know this I will not be threatened or pushed around not by you or anyone for that matter." " Sabrina, darling I wasn't threatening you, I wanted my point across to you, I don't like being doubted when I am speaking the truth I am meaning it and I was, you are beautiful to me, there nothing wrong with my eyesight. I see you just fine and I hear you, you can trust me, my dear, I am sorry that I came across as threating, I give you my word here and now I won't harm a hair on your lovely head, the punishment you get from me is a spanking, I promise?" Jack said as he crossed his heart giving her a boycott salute he was teasing to lighten the mood to get back to where they were before this dramatic moment interrupted their intense make out.

Sabrina smirked at him feeling guilty for allowing her past to interfere with her present, she needs to figure out how to not allow it to ruin her future as well.

"I wish you would tell me who hurt, so I can find them make them pay for hurting you and making it hard for me to get close to you?" Jack asked hoping to get past the wall she has built up, but Jack could tell she was ready to reveal her past to him just what she revealed which wasn't much just the who, not the how hopefully with time she will trust enough to tell him.

Right now Jack needed to get this night back on track he has to humble himself to her tread lightly. "Darling, I am so sorry, I didn't mean to scare you, it's too late to get you home, you can take the bed and I can take the couch downstairs." Jack gets off the bed then walks to the stairs to leave the room.

Then Jack felt her soft hand touch his right bicep, asked him "Wait, don't go no sense of you to sleep on that very uncomfortable couch , we can both share the bed it's big enough for both of us." asking him to stay feeling guilty for being such a drama queen when he has been nice enough bringing her here he doesn't know about her dirty past he just saw her burst from it.

"Are you sure?" Jack takes her in his squeezes it he didn't want to overstep some line here with her "yes, after all, it's your place, not mine, I am a guess here" She answered "friends?" Jack answered with a smirk trying to be smart and clever at the time.

Sabrina decided to take matters into her own hands she grabbed his face kissing him surprising each other that she would be so bold, she needed sex from this amazing and frustrating man, besides someone needed to take charge, it wasn't going to be Jack.

Then Jack picks up Sabrina carries her to the bed continuing their feasting on each other's mouths, he blindly climbs on the mattress laying her the bed continuing their make-out session when Jacks stops "Do you work tomorrow?" "no, I am off the next two days, why?" she asked "good I want you all to myself.""Do you now?" she asked flirted back "he wanted was the most handsome man that she had ever been, except the other two lovers since her break-up with Jared she quickly left the invisible presence that he had on her and she didn't want anything to stop this amazing man from doing what he wanted to do to her no matter.

Jack placed his face between her thighs she felt his warm breath on her skin so she urged him on when she whimpered "Yes" he kissed and licked the line above pubic hairline like he saving the best, he kissed and licked the lined above her pubic hairline like he was saving the best place or food for him the dessert part of her beautiful part of her lower half for last he was again taking his own sweet time which was torturing her, she wanted to take her over the edge, no this his punishment or pleasure she didn't know nor cared there was no rush for them with time on their side the rest of the world just disappeared that was just fine to them.

Sabrina felt with his very skilled fingers Jack parting her folds Sabrina was overwhelmed wanting to continue to stop with his lips along with his tongue licking he there with nerves there were sensitive she was clawing the sheets trying hard not reach down to touch him she wants this, but the need was stronger than the want it was overpowering

Sabrina was spellbound with he was doing to her, she felt the roughness and smoothness of his skin against her soft skin it was weird contrast or it felt that way to her it's been a while since she allow someone this close to her an intimate parts of her body that she hadn't allowed seeing, she hoped that she measured up the women that Jack has been within the past she wanted to please him like what he was doing to her.

Sabrina felt herself floating above them or she was exploring with the intense feeling she was having him he was still torturing her now very sensitive pussy with his fingers rubbing, the roughness of his tongue again licking her as he spreads her folds then she felt him enter her with his middle finger taking his tike again no rush to end this fucking her with his finger then he entered a second finger his pointing finger causing the intenseness to rise in her even more he would kiss her folds or then he would switch using the tip of his tongue teasing the skin or her nub it was getting so tense she almost exploided on his face she hyperventaling so much she that she would pass out he would stop placing a palm on her abs telling her to "ease into it" so she wouldn't pass out ending this love making they both didn't want that.

Jack continued his delicious torture on her he didn't care what was happening with the outside world nether did Sabrina, he was either drunk or high he wanted to take his time drinking in her sweet juices he wanted her to remember always he was there and no one else like he was branding or marking his territory.

Jack continued with his fingers as he massaged from the inside out of her interfolds teasing her like she was a toy for his pleasure he was giving her so mush pleasuring she never dreamed this moment would never to happen to her, she was afraid that she would never feel this most intense almost out of body, beautiful moment again she was so scared that it will end way too soon, but she knows in her heart and soul that she has this whatever it maybe it was too soon to start labeling this thing with Jack she won't call it love yet she didn't trust that love at first sight thing either.

Jack wasn't done yet with the playing, he began his way down her back then he nipped her cheeks she never had someone kiss and bit her ass before it felt weird and wild to her like she was the most amazing chocolate that he had ever had careful not to hurt her there with just a pinky, Sabrina didn't know if she should care that she is allowing him to claim her ass it wasn't comfortable to her mainly because she never had some one to stick their finger in her ass it was painful she was letting him know this with her painful grunts.

It was like Jack was trying to claim her in ways like every part of her beautiful body was his to do with as he pleased, she didn't stop him she didn't want to either.

Sabrina again had this push and pull to stop him like she was the most amazing chocolate he ever had. He took her juice spread them all over her folds teasing her inserted his point finger then his middle finger she felt him slide in and out of her slowly, at first then began picking up the pace with his fingers still inside of her bring her to the almost edge of her climax, but then he stopped began licking, kissing up and then nipping her skin like he can't get enough of her scent and taste of her. Then he began to feast on her mouth with his lips, as he circles his large hands around her lovely face. Jack reached over toward the nightstand beside the king sized bed that he had placed the rubbers to keep her safe from his many past lovers.

Jack rolled the condom on his large cock looking at the woman before him just lying there looking at him with such hunger in those beautiful deep blue eyes making him harden even more he placed his large member into the entrance of her core slowly at first just to see if she was ready for him oh she almost came from the a mire, touch of his head to her oversensitive then she arched her back encouraging him on with her readiness.

Jack placed his hands on the sides of her head, feasting on her lovely mouth, loving the soft moans she was making the heavy breathing he didn't want her to pass out on him, so he told her to ease into her orgasm to make it last.

Then Sabrina wrapped her long legs around Jack's waist as he continues his pace until they both felt the intense edge take over their bodies until they both let go what their bodies and souls were hungry for as they were the only ones in this crazy world getting what they wanted from each from the moment that they meet.

Sabrina couldn't believe she allowed her body to be taken by this sexy rock god making her body response in so many ways she didn't know it could do that, she didn't know Jack was this famous rock star until Julia was bragging about him almost every day she never saw his face until now here she was having the most amazing intense and mind-blowing sex with this amazing guy could have had any woman right now in his bed instead of her including Brenda

She wondered to herself what made her so different he would save her life, show her his private life his inner circle not once, but twice, now he is here feasting on her mouth other areas of her body like he was a starving who hadn't eaten in a 100 years when he has been with a hundreds of women or maybe a thousand that thought scared her was he happy with her Jack hasn't said he wasn't please maybe she needed to step up her game be more aggressive.

"Oh God that was amazing." Sabrina gasp has she and Jack fall back on the bed, trying to air in their lungs to get ready for another round of intense sex they had just shared with each other. "well your welcome my dear I aim to please." Jack answered back with a smirk trying hard not to act all cocky he has prides himself, to make sure that every woman he has been with satisfied t this was different for them both Jack and Sabrina wanted more from each other this wasn't one night stand for them.

Jack takes the rubber that was still him off, tied the end together threw it in the trash bin Jack turn toward the bed where the beautiful faced angel with her eyes closed resting for a moment he was thinking when she opened them as they stared at each other without saying a word wondering what to do next it was as if time and space as stop they weren't tired either which surprised each other how energized they were, did they want more or was this it for now.

Jack was pacing the floor after leaving the bed he turned to look at Sabrina she looked perfect laying with the white sheet covering her lovely figure her pale blonde hair pillowed around her head like it was a halo instead of angelic this time she was a pin-up or a centerfold, she had the look of hunger not for food, they will be in need some kind of food to keep up if he wanted to continue this love fest, if she was willing to stay here for the weekend until Monday.

"Come do you want to join me in the shower?" Jack asked her he didn't want their time together to stop he want to pamper and spoil her this weekend she answered him back "I would love too." he offers his hand towards her. Sabrina smiled at Jack as she took his offered hand into hers as he leads her to the bathroom was a small room with double sinks and cabinet made out of oak and cedar Sabrina could tell the cabinetry was handcrafted she wandered from the man who molded making her come several times during their lovemaking she faced the walk-in shower that was tall and wide enough for two which was perfect for them both there was the toilet on the other side of the shower.

This place felt so comfortable and cozy like it was home in fact it was a homestead many years ago as Jack explained the cabin how long it took him to finally own it was a great part of who he is when he was growing up and how he played his music Sabrina came to admire Jack the more he talks about his music how he knew that he wanted to do something in music that nothing was going to stop him from fulfilling his lifelong dream to make it in the music business Jack went on to explain how tough it was for him, in the beginning, starting with nothing after he left Midnight.

Sabrina was so surprised how relaxed she felt with Jack from not knowing to have amazing sex from almost attack that should have been a nightmare for her it was like Jack had slain some her demons from her past to their final rest when they first came to the cabin he didn't know this he allowed her to face a ghost maybe she has the strength to face the rest of her ghost too she hoped when they come for her.

Jack watched her for a moment when he noticed how quiet she become as she stood there lost in thought whatever it was he hoped that she would share that part of her no matter how dark it was he wanted to be the light to her darkened world, but he wasn't going to push until she was ready to tell her secrets, he could tell she was hiding something she had a scared look in her eyes she would be quiet like she was in her own little world somehow he wanted to do everything he can to save her from her ghosts or demons that are still haunting her like she did for him when he had to face his parents he thought he couldn't face them without her support.

CHAPTER 21

"**I**s the water too hot for you or do you want a little colder?" Jack asked seeing toward her comfort bring her back to the here and the now, Sabrina reaches in the shower to feel the water it felt wonderful to her "it is feel good to me." She smiles at him, she then stands infront of Jack, she takes him by the hand leading him into the shower stall as the warm water cascades down her head wetting her head and body, Jack then takes Sabrina's lovely face into his hands he crushes her mouth with his as he pushes her up against the wall pinning her hands above her head claiming her mouth like she was his prey he was that hungry for her he become obsessed with having her again time in the shower it was like his dick took over his mind nothing else mattered.

The fever that took over them earlier on the bed

came rushing over them as soon they hit the water as it continued to cascade down their bodies. The lovers couldn't control their bodies or minds anymore, this powerful thing that has them spelled bound like nothing else was around them not the water matter to them except for each other.

Jack still had Sabrina pinned up against the wall of the shower stall as if he was a crazy man, he feasts on her sweet delicious mouth, Sabrina thought she has died and gone to heaven Jack was her lifeline she too couldn't get enough of him either as they continue they love feast in the shower it became hot heavy for them.

Then Jack turns Sabrina to face the wall of the shower telling her to brace the wall and hold still as he kneeled down behind her, Sabrina gasp and moan as she feels his warm breath as he places soft kisses then he began licking the between the folds of her pussy teasing the nub of clicoris she has never been so licked and kissed by anyone before Jack was making sure no one else would be there after him he was spoiling her where every inch of her beautiful body was touch, kissed and licked it was overwhelming her, was thanking the heavens above this was happening her this skilled very talented more ways he cementing himself to the core of her heart hopefully to her soul too like they were meant for each other.

Sabrina felt the next wave of orgasms hit her like a freight train hard and fast, has Jack began inserting his middle finger again and then a second finger, then he continued to tease the nub with his skilled tongue until she couldn't take the extensions of her body she clasped from the most powerful orgasm yet for her, but Jack was there to catch her wrapping his arm around her tight making sure she doesn't fell to the floor of the shower, he wasn't done with Sabrina like he couldn't get enough of her he was surprised she was able to keep up his highly demanding appetite for sex the other women he has been with wanted one around of sex with him that left him frustraited and alone most of the time when he toured the country with his band, then this woman in his arms here allowing him to go crazy with, he didn't want to be selfish with her he wanted to make she can keep up with him.

Sabrina wasn't sure she could go any further, she was so born tired and so well spent she couldn't disappoint Jack she wanted this too no she needed more than anything, no she needs this more than anything. "I want to give you one more, you up for it?' He asked her "yes" she answered back "please." Jack smiled placing soft kisses on her left shoulder blade telling her how amazing he thought she was then he placed his large head of his cock near the entrance of her pussy teasing her at first causing her to beg for it "Please Jack! Stop teasing me I want more now!".

Then he entered her slowing at first then began to pick up the pace again until he almost slammed hard into her that he felt her walls tightening around his cock. Jack reached around her to wear her nub was began teasing it with his long fingers than he placed his other hand on her left nipple to tease to make it hard

Sabrina felt her body tightening again and feeling the tenseness by each body part coming alive like each one had a mind of its own because of the sensation that Jack caused with each touch and tease her body began to vibrate.

Sabrina felt her body tightening again as she felt the intense build up her body starting to lose control of her body senses like she wanted out of her body she felt her body come alive again from the teasing and caressing from Jack's fingers and hands were providing with each touch like he knew her body well where to touch her where to caress her even thou he was fulfilling his need she needed to who was the boss too not just him this can't be all about her either she needed to show she is skilled and talented too.

Sabrina felt like she was one of his guitars maybe his favorite she hoped she didn't know it sure felt like it causing her to vibrate and hum by each note he played until she couldn't hold back anymore she let the next large wave of orgasms take over her along with Jack until the strength they had before was gone then they both clasped to the floor of the shower as the water continue to cascade down their naked.

Sabrina couldn't move her body felt like liquid lead from the most powerful sex that they just shared with each other, she let Jack take care of her as he began to wash her body carefully massaging the body parts that would be sore they were too when he put pressure to them Jack had magic in his fingers when he touched a sore spot the pain just melted away Sabrina only wished he could make her other aches go away without him finding out.

With Sabrina strength returned a little she turns toward to Jack, began to wash him too she loved how hard and smooth his skin felt under her fingertips she never cared for heavy muscled men, but on Jack they were perfect like he was, Jack could tell she was enjoying the attention she was giving him she decided to give him a little taste of pleasure that he had given her twice that she felt guilty for not showing him how much he was meaning to him that she kneels down on the floor in front of Jack. She grabbed his large penis gently massaging the staff sliding up and down. She placed her mouth around the head of his penis began to suck him like he was a sucker. Jack was smooth and velvet to the touch she smiled to herself as she saw the shock and the pure pleasure on his handsome face that she was giving him that she wanted to continue until he came too, but he had other ideas like want to come inside her instead so before he reached that edge he grabbed her by the shoulders pinning her against the wall again and then he grabbed her formally by her ass causing her to wrap her long legs around his waist then he pumped her hard again until he emptied his seed into her not caring if there might be a future baby in the mix. He was overwhelmed by what she did to him that he wanted to finish with what she had started.

"You are one an amazing woman" He commented causing her to blush she wasn't used to people paying her compliments especially when she took control over him giving him a mind blowing in the shower she never did that with other men that she been with before Jack, not even Jared, she didn't know what to say to him except to say "Thank you. I aim to please" she answered shyly gaining a little bit more confidence in showing she too can play as well.

CHAPTER 22

Jack asked her to turn toward the wall he wanted to wash her beautiful hair for her, Sabrina didn't how to react to this either she has never had anyone willing to take care of her like she mattered which touched her more than anything else, so she allowed him to do what he wanted to do to her she had to admit it felt like heaven has his massaged her head with his long fingers was very gentle with his touch on her scalp a girl could get used to this..

Sabrina was being pampered from her head to her feet her whole body was humming in delight responding to his touch a soft moan escaped her lips as he continued caressing not just her hair, her whole body Jack was enjoying this too in how she was responsive to him he could tell no one in her life has ever taken charge of her being he decided that he wanted to be that person, they continued this bathroom ritual after they were rinsed off from the soap or at least, Jack did he reach around her to turn off the water he took Sabrina by the hand guiding her out of the shower he grabbed the white fluffy white towel hanging on the towel rack.

Jack began to dry and then wrapped Sabrina with the towel running his hands up and down quickly drying her hair and body Sabrina felt like he was treating her like a child she should let him know that she wasn't a child she appreciate the care he was providing her if this relationship was a boyfriend and girlfriend kind of deal it will take two to make this work this work not one sided in a sense Sabrina felt like he was doing too much for her so she took the other towel hanging on the rack she wrapped the towel around Jack too like he did for her.

Sabrina began to rub his strong arms she could feel the hard muscles that would switch underneath the terrycloth she felt the warmth of his skin her body responds to him her head began to feel her head lighten her body heat was rising she so wanted this man in all of his male beauty and what he has done to her in the shower what more he could do to her if she allows him too.

Sabrina didn't know what the future holds for her and Jack, she wanted this strong connection has with him very much she didn't know what took to make a relationship work or last she didn't have great role models when she grew-up she thinks this is why her past relationships go smoothly for her.

Sabrina hopes that Jack is the type that sticks around to help her face any storms that lay ahead of them to lay to rest the ghosts of her past ready to spring out somewhere to make her life hell, destroy the life she has made here in Midnight, she wants the life she could have with Jack if she can trust him enough to tell him the truth hoping he will be there for her not walk away from a fight that she feels heading their way. "Hey what are you thinking about," Jack asked to bring her back to the present looking at him in the bathroom mirror above the sink? "Nothing, I am fine, just worn out from all crazy sex we have been doing, you know" she lied smiling at him somewhere in his gut he feels she wasn't telling the truth which was getting to him, he didn't like being lied too or played what if she was hiding a boyfriend or worse a husband clearly somewhere in her history is haunting her now she hasn't gotten over she needs to speak her truth to him in order for them to work she just needed to know she can trust him so far its been one sided she helped him when he needed support.

"Come let's get you dried off to bed because tomorrow I am going to show you what makes this place special beside you being here, I will try to keep my hands to myself, but I can't promise" Jack teased her offering his hand toward her. "What it is?" she flirted back with a bright smile on her beautiful face she grabs the towel around his waist becoming more bolder by the moment it must be the Jack effect the longer she is around him the more bold and daring she is getting she is enjoying this, but he stops her from taking his towel he wiggled his fingers at her told her "behave, it's called a surprise." he teased in a sexy tone causing her to pout batting her eyes at him, he won't cave to her charm which she didn't think she had much of, so she glared at him shaking her head at him as he takes her by the hand with them both still wrapped in towels realizing that there weren't many clothes for her to sleep in he offered her a white t-shirt of his. The shirt looked like a dress on her that came to her knees she was complaining, any girl would wine and moan about not having their clothes and make-up, Sabrina didn't Jack is coming to respect her, she was a strong woman Jack didn't think she knew that or wasn't a wear of that fact about herself she does have a lot of self-doubt about her he could sense he might have to help her out with that, she wasn't caught up in the girly stuff that most women that Jack has come across over the years playing in the clubs and the concert halls he has traveled he didn't come to care for the drama and the mind games that filled their daily lives this would make his head spin it made him leary of women would who would follow him in general that is why he kept his distance while he traveled his way to stardom but with Miss Parker here there was something different about her she was real, he knows she isn't forthcoming about her past that he isn't liking, he wanted her to come to him when she was ready he didn't want to rush her and her beauty was all natural had him spell bound that has him hooked this was Sabrina.

Jack was worried about what has this beautiful woman scared that as her ready to jump out of her skin or run, he wants to be there for her no matter what ahead of them he just wished she would trust him, he guessed almost saving her life wasn't enough for her that he was trustworthy maybe it wasn't just with him thou maybe it started with someone else of her past has hurt her badly he wasn't sure, he would have to do more than save her to gain her trust. Sabrina was such a good-hearted woman who would hurt her so easily, she has come to mean a great deal to him.

Jack just needed to be a little patient towards her let her know that he was here for her like she was there for him when he needed more encouragement with his parents he needed to give her the same he just wished he knew what he could do to show that she could trust him in order for him to do that was to show her or tell her, he could tell she wasn't shown a lot of compassion in her life that saddens him he can't figure out why someone would mistreat her, he needed to show she was safe with him.

Tomorrow Jack needed to show her that he cared about her he couldn't use the word love for her, but he knows he would do anything for he didn't know if that was love like what he saw in his folks, he wanted to continue to show her she can trust him in order for him to do that he wanted to take her to show what makes this property so important for him to buy when he came rich he can keep safe why this place holds a special place in his heart more than the beach house and cabin that he discovered one summer and when he needed a safe place to go to after his huge fight with his parents, he made sure that the area he wants to show Sabrina was part of the sale when he bought the cabin.

CHAPTER 24

'*The rain is pounding on the ground hard matching heartbeat and heavy breathing, as Sabrina runs through the darkened woods not knowing where he was "is he coming where was he, I hear him screaming for me", she had to get out before he catches her she still running continuously she is living a nightmare she can't escape, she hear him getting closer she doesn't know where to go she must flee she was never more scared in her life Sabrina feels herself tripping over a log or something she didn't know what, the sharp pain landing hard on the ground with her knee Jared's disembodied voice barking at her that she was a died woman if he caught up with her he was there behind her running towards she had to get up, but she can't move she is frozen. She hears herself breathing hard she tries to get up she can't get up he has a gun in hand he fires the rain is pouring there is silence."*

then a loud clap of thunder startled Sabrina awake, she arose up quickly she was soaked from the sweat, she trying to calm her beating heart from the nightmare that she had, she looks around her quickly to see if it was real and not her dream then she remembered where she was and with whom she was with she looks to her left eyeing the still sleeping, gorgeous form of Jack, when she heard the rumbling of thunder outside in the distance that caused her to hurry out of bed wrapping a rob that she found in a chair, she was facing her nightmare again, this time it was a different place with a different man the nightmare felt so real to her, in fact, she was still shaking from it she stretched out her fingers to see to watch them shake that man in the bed wasn't evil thou the one who is is still looking for her he won't stop until he finds her.

Sabrina rushed down the stairs goes to the large window facing the living room of the cabin, through the dim light of the mid-night moon the wind was blowing the trees about like a madman was shaking them trying to end their breathing like her nightmare coming true she didn't want to be there but she had to be for Jack's sake then Sabrina open the door to look outside as an eerie chill filled her vanes, she circled her arms around to ward off the chill, Sabrina decided there she won't let past control her future thou somewhere out there her past is waiting for her, she just didn't know when, but she feels it will be soon.

Sabrina quietly crawls back into bed, she feels Jack warmth as his strong arm wrapped around her giving her the comfort she needed without knowing or too half asleep to notice her trembling she stopped when she snuggled up to him to get warm again she looks over her shoulder at Jack she whispered to him "I love you "she would do anything to keep what they are building here safe no matter what it cost her.

Jack watches the beauty in his bed right now he never felt this strongly for a woman he barely knew he didn't dare himself to believe Sabrina could be the one he would be willing to show her the most sacred place he has never taken anyone in his life before not even his parents know of the cabin, not even the most secret he is about to share with Sabrina, the beach house he should show them before too long he can't hide his prize processions from them show off his success in the music business has given especially to his Pop.

Jack continued to gaze at the lovely woman still sleeping in his bed looked like she was at peace like an angel with her pale blonde hair looks like the sun had kissed leaving its rays or marks on each and every strain of hair he loved her killer body which was covered by the white top sheet c just a thought of her without anything on caused his cock to harden then his mind went to why she got up earlier he felt her leave quickly like she was running from something or someone after a clap of thunder and hard rain he didn't know if it was a dream or nightmare she was having he didn't know he wanted to go after her in case she left, but then felt her climb back to bed she was shaking he felt the need to comfort her as he wrapped his arm around he didn't think she knew he was awake the whole time he didn't know how to help her, he did feel her relax when he put his arm around her he could tell that was the only thing she needs he was happy that he provides that for her, but soon he will have to ask her what was going on with her and soon.

Jack didn't want to wake her, but he wanted to get this today started because he wanted to show her his next surprise, he hoped she would love it like he did, he wanted her to see what makes not just this cabin magical also the woods as well too not just for the peaceful setting, also for the beauty which is pale in comparison to the woman still sleeping and covered in the white sheet now her beautiful tits were exposed to him, he loved them when he touched them several times during the night with their marathon of sex and making love in the bed and in the shower, he resisted the temptation her right tit he wanted to make her nipple hard and then suck it just a thought of this made him hard.

Jack got caught up in the moment he didn't think he was in the moment kind of guy, but he started it he had to continue by placing a soft kiss on her mouth he placed his lips on her tip causing her to moan awake continuing their lovemaking like it never stopped for them.

Moments later after their incredible lovemaking Jack wondered what was her secrets were that she needed to hide them from him he could sense that something has her scared from her spooked look on her face was not just from her near-rape it has to do with the cabin he didn't think she ever been here before he was the one who brought them here to get away from Brenda's hold on him, something didn't feel right to him about this whole situation he needed to solve it and soon before they get to close, but he told himself he would let her come to him when she was ready and was comfortable around him.

CHAPTER 25

J ack studies the red rose for a moment then at the lovely rose in his bed whose beauty makes the flower in his hand look pale in comparison, he quietly got into the bed to get closer to Sabrina without waking her, Jack takes the rose by the steam tipping the full bloom of the rose toward her forehead caressing her body with the bud of the rose trying to awake her which worked when her eyes flutter open she turned her face to look him with a smile.

"Morning beautiful" Jack places soft kisses on the tips of her breasts that sent a delicious current through her vanes, then he kissed her beautiful lips giving her an amazing good morning kiss that curled her toes bring her fully awake "wow what a kiss" she asked blushing from head to toe, Sabrina was acting so shy around she didn't know why he has seen her nake and allowed him to do some an amazing things with her, they haven't had their first date or does this whole cabin or maybe his beach house was she wasn't sure.

Then Sabrina looks up to see Jack carrying a tray full of food that he had made for him and her, she never felt so pampered before, it was always her that made the effort show she cared she guessed why she didn't have a lot of men in her life they always wanted something from her just not her period she is very touched by Jack's kindness toward her, but she was still leary of any kindness given to her.

After breakfast, come let's get the rest of the day started I have a surprise for you" Jack with a bright smile that said he was up to something he offered his hand toward her, she couldn't help but smile at him then took his offered hand as he pulled her off the bed.

Sabrina needed to do something for Jack to show him how much she appreciated him she was really grateful to him for he has done so much for her more than most people would do in a week she was in awe of him if only he would release control he had over their relationship if that what this is she wasn't sure what to call this thing Jack and her maybe she should be bold come out ask what he sees for them was he too afraid to label what this was between them or was she reading too much into this picture she did wanted to make this thing work for them both she couldn't put a name to it yet, then she thought she would have to bend the rules and be sneaky he didn't have to know until afterwards this caused a smile form on her face that she too can be in control to.

"What are you smiling about?" Jack watched getting ready for their walk in the woods then he realized she went quiet for a moment he thought "oh no not another dark memory was resurfacing again," then he turned to look at to see what was happening instead of a dark cloud, there was a ray of sun shine with a smile spreading across her smile she didn't answer him with words, but a soft and hot kiss that his cock almost stood up and hard, she stopped the kissing walked toward the stairs "Ready?" she teased without saying anything further about the kissed and why she was smiling, he knows she was up to something this time it was good he hoped.

CHAPTER 26

Jack and Sabrina walked a trail leading somewhere Sabrina wasn't sure Jack was very vague in describing where they were heading. It was a crisp beautiful morning slowly turned into day they held hands and talked about their lives before each other met.

Sabrina was careful with what she revealed to him before she came to Midnight which wasn't good compared to his life with his parents this him sad for her, she seemed so put together and happy now all her focus is on her life is now she couldn't afford to think what life was, the past didn't the bills she made up her mind that she would leave New Kirk and never look back, just look ahead, what surprised her the most about this little hike they were on how Jack got up early to go into town to buy her some clothes and shoes that fit he sought out her comfort than his, she promised to pay him back for them he won't have it they were a gift.

Sabrina wasn't comfortable being spoiled like this or center of attention with what she has been through when men before Jack, she asked him about his music the tours that he went on, talked about his favorite on the planet was New York, how real and lively it was there was so much to do you couldn't fit New York in one trip you would have to spend a month, maybe a year to see all of New York.

Sabrina continued to look around her all she saw were the trees surrounding them wondering what the surprise was that has him was so excited to show, then she started to hear rushing waters that were getting louder as they got closer to where the sounds were coming from, then they came to a clearing.

Sabrina just stood in awe with what she was seeing the most breathtaking sight before her was a towering waterfall cascading down the heavy cliffs, the falls weren't the giants like Nigeria or Shoshone falls they were tall to her, the forces of nature before her was overwhelming to her she almost forgot about Jack's presence until she felt Jack's arms circle around her neck causing her to stiffen up a little, then she relaxed some when she felt his warm breath on her skin, in a hushed voice " what do you think of this?" he asked "Oh Jack there are no words with what I am seeing I thought the beach was amazing this is beyond breathtaking!!" she gushed with a large smile that spread across her beautiful face making Jack felt proudful that showing this was the right choice he made.

The waterfall cascaded down from the creek above them that emptied into the pool that was before them.

"Come?" Jack quickly grabbed Sabrina by the hand as they walked closer to the falls, she could see that there was a cave that hidden behind the falls there was a rocky path that lead behind the falls as she got closer to the falling water that the darkness of the cave that the falls hidden was Jack's was the surprise for her, but was hidden in the cave was another level. Then Jack took a flash light out of his back pack turning it to show the deepness of the cave and the walls were covered from roof to the walls crystal like quartz the walls looked like glittery rainbow, towards the back of the cave was a flat surface that had a sleeping bag and a pillow with latern, Jack takes a book of matches that he fished from his backpack that he had taken off placing by the sleeping bag. Sabrina looked at Jack with new eyes, he wasn't just a rock god to millions of women, but he was also a mountain man underneath too. He could survive anything if he put his mind to it, she liked that about him too, plus he loves his family, hopefully he liked her or seems he wouldn't have brought her to share what matters to him, she so wanted to believe that she did matter to him. "Hey what are you thinking about about, come here and sit next to me?" Jack ask as he pats the empty spot on the sleeping bag that he was sitting crossed legged on right now. Jack reached up offering his hand toward Sabrina, then she took it kneeling down on the sleeping bag next to Jack wondering what to do next, but then she looked up scanning the cave that surrounded them trying figure out the place because there were just rocks, the quartz that was sticking out of the walls that look like a rainbow she was instantly impressed with everything around them, "what do you think? You like?!" Jack asks hoping that the woman before him was impressed with what she saw because he really wanted to impress her.

Jack so wanted this lovely woman before him to care about what he holds dear to him, that there was more to him then his music, his money and fame. Sabrina didn't seem to care about all that, Jack like that a lot about her that she asked about his music in general, what made him choice music in the first place, what did he like the most about the music that he made was watching people move, laugh and smile, just wanted his fans to have fun and they got their money worth.

"Jack this is amazing place, I like it here I see why you like it here. This place is very peaceful and so is the cabin. How long have you own this place?" she asked him Jack answered her back "Not long. Has soon I got the money I made sure that these places were ready for me to buy."

Jack takes a hammer and a pick to take a chuck of quartz that was a deep blue that match the color of Sabrina's eyes. Jack held the rock up to her face and said "this rock matches the color of your eyes" that caused her to blushed, Jack thought that was adorable that he could make her blush a little and that she doesn't takes her looks all to serious like the women that seem to want the money and the fame, that matters more to them than it does to her Jack like that about her a lot when he looks at Sabrina right of him, he can see that she was a honest woman even if looks can be deceiving, but she hasn't done anything so far to be dishonest with, he could tell that she is holding something back because she gets so lost in thought and quiet.

When they first came to the cabin, she had a scared as if she was looking at ghost with the haunted look she had on her face and when he asked her if she was okay, she gave a small smile that didn't reached her eyes answered him that she was was okay, but he is trying to be patient with her. Jack wanted to tell her that she could trust him that no matter what happens he will be there for her and that she didn't needed to be afraid of anything. Sabrina gave him courage to meet his fears head on by meeting his parents. He wanted to give her that same courage with whatever fears that she is facing so that she didn't have to face them a lone. He wished he could tell her that without him overstepping the invisible boundary that divides them from heading forward, but they haven't had any fights yet to see if they can face the troubles that might face them.

Jared stares at the t.v. of his hotel room plotting his next move to destroy his ex-Sabrina life for good, thinking he could use the lovely Brenda, she did seemed edger to help him to getting even with his ex because she believe, Sabrina stolen her Jack right from under her nose and she would do anything to help get him back no matter the cost to her. She doesn't know what that it may cost her maybe her freedom better, yet it may cost her life as well Jared hoped it wouldn't come to that, but if he had to keep his secrets hidden, he will have to ends lives here he didn't care. If he played his cards right, he could get what he wants and deserved.

Jared is hell bent on making sure that he finally gets what he wanted, when this journey ends for him. If he had to kill to do it so, be it. Jared already lost a great deal of time and money on searching for his ex the little slut he didn't think she could attract anyone let lone someone like Jack "who knew what the boy liked in women which wasn't much, but he turned Brenda down flat which he didn't understand because she was the whole package to him with her big hair and tits, Yeah they were faked." he didn't care, but he was certain thou he was going to back sure that Jack sees Sabrina as not the angel that she appears to be even he had to lie a little to make her look bad he wants the revenge. When Jared is sure that Sabrina's doesn't have anyone to help her. Then he will attack she won't see it coming until it is too late, then he will make sure that she doesn't breathe again when he is done, but he wants to make sure all his ducks at in the row for him to set his game to action. He just needs to use Brenda and someone else as bate to lore Sabrina out of hiding. Jared let a smile spread across his face as the plot for revenge began to take place in his mind all he had to do was to reach out to the lovely Brenda. Jared looks at the piece of paper that had the sweet minx number on it to see if she was serious about helping him to get even with Sabrina and then everything else will play out on its own. He just had to by his time, he also needed to get something information from Brenda, where Sabrina live and what her number maybe start haunting her to make her know that he had find her, that she isn't seeing a ghost that he was real, this time he will finished what he didn't get to do the last time that they saw each other in the woods. The sound of thunder could be heard outside in the distance Jared got up off the bed, walked over to the large bay window that looked out toward the parking lot of the hotel that he was staying at he saw the lightening flashing in the sky above him and the thunder was rumbling quiet warning those around that the storm was coming so was the storm that was coming for Sabrina too. Jared thought to himself, but then he saw the mountains top wondered to himself if there were cabin up there for him use too that would be perfect for him to set the scene to everyone including his ex. Jared thought about the timing how perfect it would be for him to get all that was stolen from him and he would ride off into the sunset with all his hard work done with Sabrina's life finally in ruin and/or better yet her life in ruin, her life over with there no one there to save her would be perfect no one would have to know that it was him that killed her all he have to do was dial this number it will be all over for Sabrina. Jared took the receiver from the cradle of the telephone began to finger punched the buttons after he heard the dial tone, then he heard the purred voice of Brenda come over the receiver then a smile began to spread across his and then he felt his cock began to harden with the sound of her voice. He wondered if she wouldn't mind having a quickie with him. "It wouldn't hurt" he thought, and it would make him feel better thou, in the end she was willing to come over to think of a plan for them to get even with Sabrina. He also wanted to know if she wanted to spend the night with him, but she wasn't sure she wanted to mix business with pleasure. Old Jared doesn't take no for an answer if he had to do some forcing then so be it, Brenda will be under him in no time, when she gets here.

Jack and Sabrina stayed in the cave until the rain had pasted, as they laid on the sleeping bag, they continued the make out session that they had in the bedroom of the cabin. Jack never wanted this time with Sabrina to end and neither did Sabrina, she wanted this time to go on forever. She was so enjoying the time that they were having like they were becoming one in their bodies as well their souls no matter what was happening outside those woods that she didn't want to let go with this very personal, physical connection that they were share that she was afraid that soon the outside world that surrounded them right now "god this was amazing!" Sabrina thought as they lay there in silence for a moment not daring to move in fear if she did things would change between them, they didn't want that. "That was the most amazing thing" Jack also thought in silence as they enjoyed the sound of the rain coming down, to Sabrina amazement she wasn't scared of the rain like she use to be, thanks to the most amazing man that was continual his kissing on her in that cave like they were home than any other place. They both were laying on their side as they gazed at one other, Then Jack reach over began caressing the soft skin of Sabrina's cheek wondered to himself what she did to her skin to make it so soft and perfect he knows that there are models out there that would give almost anything to have the flawless complexion that Sabrina, she works at the diner with all that grease go figure, then Jack placed a soft kiss on her lips again as he covers her beautiful body with his and then he placed his hands around her lovely face he told her that she was the most creature that he ever saw which caused her to blushed further not believing what he had to say he had to see the flaws that were there, but maybe if he didn't see it was a good thing that he didn't see the flaws underneath because if he did see them he would run away or something. Sabrina would not allow anyone to see those flaws if she could help it the people that saw them told her that they saw them "what are you thinking about?" Jack asked with concern in his voice "nothing, just that you need to have your eyes checked because you're seeing things." Sabrina answered back as she lay underneath him still enjoying this time with Jack. "Darling, I see you just fine, there is nothing wrong with my eyes, thank you" Jack said with a smirk as he gathered her up in his arms and then leaned against the rocky wall of the cave. Sabrina like the fact that Jack was a cuddlier especially after making love which was okay with her it made this moment with Jack more special to her it made her feel cherished, she never had that before with anyone she was with especially Jared, she quickly dashed him out of her head she didn't want the thought of that man ruining this moment with Jack. Sabrina just wished that Jared would just disappear for good she didn't want her past to come and ruin her future, the closer she gets with Jack as she continue to lay in his strong arms feeling safe right now, but she knew that somewhere out there Jared wouldn't rest until he got what he wanted from her. Sabrina couldn't bare to face what the future held for her, but she knew that she wanted a future with Jack if she could help it. "Hey Babe, what is wrong you have been so lost in thoughts from the moment we have been here?" Jack asks not taking the silent scared look on Sabrina's anymore and wanting the truth from her this time. as he placed a hand on the side of her face looking at her with those blue eyes that held more than they should. "Jack, I am fine, I know I should tell you what is going on inside of me, but I can't right now not until I am ready." "okay, I will let this slide just once, I want answers from you, I don't like secrets, the longer they are the more they ruin the lives once they are reveals and it takes a long time for those lives to be repaired. I have seen them trust me, I have" Jack muttered to her "I understand that, but right now I can't tell my secrets yet, there no big deal thou nothing to worry about. I promise" Sabrina almost lying to herself too. As she looks around her trying to get them off the subject of her and her secrets. Jack not believing what she was telling him right now, but he backed off for the moment, but his trust in her is weakening just a little, which was saddening to him right now because he thought he had found the one woman other his mother that he could trust, he thought he was wrong, hopefully there was still a chance for them to make it past the mistrust that was forming real quick right now, it scared him right now because he cares so much for her and that he would do almost anything for her whatever the demons that scared her life before him. He wants to save her and protect her from, but if she doesn't trust him enough to share them with her then what should he do without forcing her to confess them. Jack is in unfamiliar territory here where a female doesn't feel save enough to trust him but is willing to give her body to him. Jack was hoping she was willing to give me her heart as well as he was willing to give his heart to her. Sabrina saw the cloud that was in Jack's eyes got scared that if she didn't do anything at that moment, she was going to lose the best thing that has ever happened to her, and she didn't want that no matter what she had to think to get him to believe her again. "Hey Jack, don't worry, there is nothing to worry about okay. I am fine, I just think too much sometimes of stupid things that happened to me a long time ago that have nothing to do with us. I promise!" she lied a little, then began kissing him again trying to get him to smile a little and then she throws her arms around his neck and then she felt his arms engulfing her pulling her in closer to him. Then he kissed her hard that the soft kisses that he used to give like he was trying to branding her with his mouth. Then Jack pined Sabrina to the sleeping bag again with a hard look on his handsome face " I will let this slide just this once, but I will not be played for a fool again I want the truth from you do I make myself clear" Jack snapped letting her to see the hurt in his eyes all that he has done for her, by showing her the secrets places that were his sanctuary and his home, his heart to her, most importantly he saved her life when he could have let her fend for herself when those three fuckers who were trying to have her for dessert of course he wouldn't let anything to happen if he knew now compare to then, but still it started to get annoying to him to for the way what he was thinking and feeling right now. He didn't like the way things are heading right now, if she didn't start talking about what was bothering her. He didn't think there would be much of a future with Sabrina. Jack got up; from her he quickly got his clothes on him without looking at her. Sabrina just stared at Jack with a sadden look, that got her scared because she didn't know what to do here, this was foreign to her, she had never had to worry about hurting someone else's feelings, just hers. She watched marched to the opening to the cave and then he turned to look at her "are you coming" Jack commanded causing Sabrina to jump a little she hurried to get dressed to catch up with as they walked in silences for a moment.

Then Jack stopped turn toward Sabrina placing his hands around her face admiring the pure beautiful of this woman that almost captured his soul along with his heart. Jack didn't want to give up what they were building her, but what cost her secrets would be for him. If he got further into their relationship, would he lose everything including his heart and his soul too, could he pick up the pieces that were left and move on. Jack placed his lips on Sabrina's sweet mouth as well, pulling her in closer to him, as he deepened the kissed trying hard to keep this cherished moment from spinning out of control as it was "Please, darling tell me your secrets that has you so scared that when you see a cabin, you see a ghost. You can trust me I will do anything to protect you from your demons, please I am trying to be patient here, we can't move forward if we can't get past the secrets and the lies" Jack begged which he never done to a woman pegging her. Sabrina wanted to cry in that moment as she looks at this amazing man that was begging her to trust him and she did trust him in that moment, but she couldn't bring the truth out yet she couldn't bare the fall out if she did, losing the one person that have come to mean so much to her in the short amount of time that they have known each other. "I have no demons I promise just that my life hasn't been easy and some places such as the cabin bring back bad memories for me that is it. There are no secrets that I am hiding from you, I promise" Sabrina said in a half truth manner. She reaches up on her tiptoes placing a soft kiss on his cheek, then Jack wrapped his arms around her body trying to hold unto her beautiful body and this amazing thing that they have been building, but her half truths that he is still not feeling the truth from her, his gut is telling him that there is something else that she is hiding from him, he wonder if to himself what he is holding unto is worth losing himself in this thing that he can't put his finger on yet.

"Darling I am going to give you the benefit of doubt of doubt here, but if you are lying about something that is important that I should know about then I am done with you there is no going back once my trust is broken, do I make myself clear here" Jack commanded making sure he was clear here that no one is going to make him look the fool, he has been there and done that.

Jack swiftly scoops Sabrina up throwing her on his shoulder like she is a sack of potatoes causing her to squeal and screamed "Ouch" when he swot her on the behind, he marched onto the cabin, up the steps that lead to the bedroom and then he throws her onto the bed. He pinned her again the bed, he began to feast onto her lips, Jack never tasted the sweetest lips to him as he tasted Sabrina's lips. Jack wanted this moment for them to last forever until the real world comes knocking for them and changing them forever for good. Jack didn't know what was in store for them, but he knew that this moment needed to be special for him and her. So, Jack took his sweet time her placing soft kisses on her forehead, then her nose, and her cheeks. Sabrina felt like she was in heaven with Jack as he began to kiss her, she didn't know what the future held for them now, but she needed to make this moment for them, to last forever, that is why she wasn't in a hurry to end this with Jack. They both rushed to pull off their clothes because they didn't want anything between their needs for each other and their hungry bodies that weren't hungry for food. They continued with their kissing, then Jack placed hot kisses on Sabrina's nibbles and sucking them causing her to arch her back, begging him that she want, no needed more than this from him. Jack sensing her silent needed that she was craving that he was making her feel that her body with demanding him to fill. Jack placed his hot mouth down her stomach down toward the line of her pubic hair that covered her sensitive mound. Jack took his skilled fingers that knew how to please a woman such as Sabrina was in need of release that was building up inside her when she felt his finger began to caress her there causing her insides to tense up wanting and needing him to finish with whatever he is doing to her, but no, he wanted this to be slow, lasting. Jack finds her opening as he slowly slides his middle finger inside as he placed his still hot lips on her swollen clip, and he used his skilled tongue on her sensitive pussy. Sabrina didn't know if this was sweet hell that she was in or hot heaven. Sabrina placed her hands on Jack's head encouraging him to continue his sweet torture as Sabrina watched him given her pleasure. Sabrina thought that the first time they had sweet the sex was amazing this was coming to be mind blowing, out of the world love making that she didn't want to end. "Jack, I am going to come, please I need more" She begged rapturing and whimpered as he continued with his sweet torture instead of one finger, he placed two fingers inside her and he also continue with his teasing of her clit with his tongue picking up his speed wanting her to come on his lips. Jack wanted to get drunk off her sweet juices as they flowed out of her as Sabrina came hard. She didn't know if she could take more from this amazing man was giving her so such more that it almost made her sweep that she didn't want this to end. "I love you Jack, please don't stop I need you.!" she shouted back as his slide his large cock inside without the protection of condom that he should have put on him, but he didn't want anything between them just skin on skin. It felt like heaven to him especially with what she shouts out that she loved him deeply that she needed this with him and so did he.

CHAPTER 29

Jack and Sabrina stood outside the Diner the next morning after the amazing weekend, get a way that they had shared from where they started from when they left the Diner with Brenda screaming after Jack to now, with them both so happy and content they didn't want anything to end, but the real world could not wait, even thou they didn't want to face what the real world had in store for them, even thou at the time they didn't know what that might be or how soon it will be. They were so content to be with each other and be happy with their little world that they had made. They didn't want the rest of the world messing up or interfering with their lives, even those that are out there or in the diner would gladly come between them. Sabrina just hope that their newfound love was strong enough to with stand the storm that is head of them. Sabrina needed time to tell the truth to Jack before the world tells their verison of the truth to him. "Hey why don't you go in first. I needed to make a phone call first, okay" Jack ask giving her reassuring smile that anything with is okay even thou deep down inside, Jack's know something isn't right with Sabrina, she is lost in her mind like she worried about something that she is afraid to tell him or something.

Jack places a sweet kiss on Sabrina lips, before she turns toward the glass door, she turns to look at him with a smile on her face and then grabs the handle of the door pushes open the glass door and walks into the diner lobby.

The Diner was busy for this Monday morning, but for some reason something felt off for Sabrina like something wasn't right. Sabrina did not want to be she did know why, she wanted to be somewhere else with Jack.

"Hey, if you wanted your presences known, you better get your sweet ass here" Brenda purred over the office phone "great see you soon, I can't wait to see her face, I wished I had a camera to cherish the look on Sabrina face when she sees you. If there is anything I can do to help, oh okay, I will be there, can't wait to see you!" Brenda asks cheerfully "who are you talking too?" Julia asks, coming into the office that caused Brenda to jump a little. She turned to see Julia with her arms folded in front of her and tapping her foot to the ground, with a sheepish grinned on her face, Brenda said "no one, just a friend on the phone" she lied to Julia, hoping that she would believe Brenda , which Julia didn't because Brenda doesn't have friends. Julia could tell that she was up to something because when Sabrina came into the diner Brenda rushed to the office like her tail was on fire and now, she was talking to a secret friend. Julia didn't trust Brenda not as far as she could throw her, she needed to keep an eye on Brenda.

Moments later the crowd in the diner began to wine down. Sabrina was at the counter table just talking to Jack and another gentleman that was chatten away. When Sabrina felt someone's eyes on her that caused her to look up, she sees him outside or she thinks she sees someone that looks like Jared then Sabrina's worst fears have come true that he has finally found her. "Oh my god, no!" She gasped as the dish that she had in her hands slips and falls to the floor splitting into pieces just like her perfect little world in that moment until she looks up, through the window like time stood still for her and then she got frighten and then he wasn't there again. "Wow Sabrina, my dear, you look like you have seen a ghost." Brenda smirked at Sabrina loving the terrior look at her face, giving her a knowing look that told Sabrina, that Brenda knows about Jared and that her worst fears have come true for her. Sabrina felt her world that she had struggled so hard to rebuild for her is coming apart in a heart beat, she felt trapped like there was no way out for her except to run toward the back to get some air so she could breath again and figure what to do next. Sabrina storms toward the back wanting to be free again she knows she can't until she deals with Jared once and for all, out in the back where the cast iron park bench was, Sabrina sink onto the bench trying to catch her breath, her tears started to flow down her cheeks uncontrollably.

Jack sees the scared look on Sabrina lovely face as she looks outside towards the window, Jack turns to the window to see what she is looking at, but didn't see anything just an empty space between the parked car in front of the window there was someone or something that brought horrified look on her lovely face that had he concern and then he hears Branda's responses to Sabrina's scared look too, like she knows something then he sees Sabrina let the plate in her hands slip through her hands and rushed towards the back that caused him to get up to follow her towards the backyard of the diner to see what was going on with Sabrina and he founding her shacking and crying over something she saw outside in the front of the diner he didn't see anything that might have frighten her. "Darling, tell me what you has so frighten. You look pale like you seen a ghost" Jack pleaded for her to tell him the truth so he can help her or do something.

Sabrina throws herself into his arms, scared, not knowing what to do, she couldn't tell him the truth, but she needed to say something to him. She didn't want Jack involved whatsoever, with what Jared had planned for her, she knowns it wouldn't be good. Jack pleaded with her tell him what was going on, that she can trust him to help whatever it is, but she was too scared to ask for help and she couldn't risk anyone especially Jack getting hurt because Jared would use anyone especially those, she cared about against her. Sabrina has fallen in love with Jack, if Jack knew what happen or what she has done he would turn his back on her like her father did all those years ago when she was young, without second thought. She can't risk being hurt again by him or anyone. Sabrina felt the walls were moving in on her and she needed to leave " Jack, I needed to leave, tell your mom that I am not feeling well that I needed to go home, please" Sabrina begging him for help and not asked questions even thou he had the right to know the truth, but she couldn't tell him right now, she places a lone kiss on his cheek, as if she is telling him goodbye. Then she leaves from the tall wooden fence that protects the back of the diner, with perfect timing the town bus shows up, and Sabrina hurries to get on it, then she looks back to see Jack walking fast towards the bus stop, in shock to see her leave Jack is confused with what was going on than feels Brenda approached him from the behind telling him telling that he needed to hear her out why Sabrina had ran the way she did "Jack, you need to know about Sabrina, she isn't the angel that she appears, but she is married this man Jared Smith, she ran away from him when she was younger after she tried to kill him!" Brenda said to him and then she handed him an old picture of Sabrina and Jared when they were together, they looked like a happy couple in the picure. Jack didn't know who was telling him the truth "no your lying, she isn't married no she never said she was married" Jack said then thought back when Sabrina would be lost in thoughts or when she would have a scared look on her face when she laid her eyes on the cabin and when he felt her tremble when there was a storm outside of the cabin, when she thought he was a sleep.

Sabrina looks back again, thinking this might be the last time she would be seeing him and with horror she sees Brenda coming up behind he turns towards her as Sabrina sees Brenda telling him something, Sabrina sees them disappear from her view when the bus starts to pull away.

As Julia watches the actions between Jack and Brenda , she did not want that woman's claws to digging into her son's skin if she can help it, Julia watches Brenda rushing towards her car door opens and slides into the car, after she sees Brenda chatting with her son. Julia did not like the look on his face like he was punch in the his gut. Julia was going to protect her son at all costs. Julia follows Brenda in her car to a rundown hotel and sees Brenda get out of her care and enters a room, then a gun and a gloved hand comes through the window covering her mouth.

CHAPTER 30

Sabrina rode the bus all over the town trying to figure how to get out of this mess she was in, she is going to need to face this head somehow later in the day she approaches her apartment building when she sees Jack's form on the steps of the stairwell that leads up to the second floor appartments. Sabrina feared the cold, but concerned look on his face, she didn't know what to say to him "Hi" she finally said after a moment of pure silence between them not knowing what to say like their were back, being strangers again "who is Jared Smith? Is he your husband like Brenda is claiming him to be?" Jack asked her, feeling like his has been ran over by a mad truck of emotions wanting to believe that Sabrina wasn't lying to him, or that Brenda was being her typical revengeful self trying to get to him or going after Sabrina because of him, he didn't know, but he needed the answers. Sabrina steps towards the door of one bedroom, bathroom apartment, without responding to his questions which was driving him crazy right now because his heart and his pride was hanging by a thread that was getting ready to snap any second, if she doesn't answer him, he didn't like this feeling of being out of control especially with those around him that he loves more than this woman before him seems to be liking the torture she was giving without seeming understand that, she is still not giving relief that he seeks.

Sabrina can't read Jack's facial expressions on his handsome, but she can see that whatever Brenda told him about Jared, Sabrina could feel the tension from him that you could cut it with the knife, she wants to speak the truth and Jack deserves that the truth after all she owes him her life and much more, but right now she just can't bring herself to speak the truth that he is seeking.

Sabrina allows Jack's to enter into her apartment, the first thing you see when you enter the small apartment is the wooden the sliding door to the coat closet, then turn towards the left the leads to is the kitchen and very spacious living room which the sitting table that is left just past the kitchen counter, there is a tall bamboo planet that is by the sliding door that leads onto the wooden balcony, with a small patio set that was made out of black metal, facing the large bay window was her overstuffed brown leather couch and the large hall that has coat close was the black metal theater set that has her 19 inch screen tv. and on the left was the Bathroom and her bedroom Jack was assuming but has him scared right now is how little there is in personal touch that looks like anyone could be living here, not a single female or he thought she was single he didn't know because she still hasn't answered his questions which was killing him right now.

Sabrina remained silent as their moved further into the apart, scared with what to say to the man to has come dear to him, but truth refuses to escape her lips, with Jared here getting ready to strike any moment "So is it true are you married?" Jack demand again trying hard not to explode in angrier with the woman that has come to mean more to him then anyone.

As if on cue the phone rings for no reason at all for being annoying them because they are in the middle of something important, but instead of ignoring the stupid contrapation like Jack had hoped she would they need to have this talk that could make or break their relationship. Sabrina grabbed the damn phone bring the receiver toward her right ear and frozed when she heard the familiar voice of Jared come through the phone "long time no see, Bitch! Tell lover boy to leave or I will put a bullet through his mother's head, Speak old woman!" Jared glared over the phone then a cold chili ran through Sabrina body when she heard, Julia terrified voice come through the phone, just making sure Sabrina knew that Jared meant business "Sabrina, help me, please!" Julia cried over the phone then she heard a big bang of gun going off could be going off in the back ground "tell him to leave and don't say a word that his mother is in trouble, or the next bullet will go into her!" Jared demanded.

Sabrina turned, placing the receiver on her chest as she looked at Jack pleading silenctly for him to help her, but didn't, "Jack, its my father on the phone he wants to speak about something important, can we talk about this later, please" Sabrina pleaded with him to leave so she could listen to what Jared wanted and figure out how to help Julia out on her own. "Fine, I will leave, but this isn't done" Jack demand pointed between them both. Then Jack stalked towards her taking her face into his large hands wanting to wring her neck, but instead Jack crushed his lips against hers making her feel the storm of emotions that he was feeling or was he claiming her or saying goodbye to Sabrina she couldn't tell, she grabbed onto this one last kiss as if it was her life line she needed to hang onto something to give her the strength to get throught whatever Jared has instore for her and her guest wasn't good. Then Sabrina sees Jack turn stalking towards the door and walk through without looking back, Sabrina, felt her heart break into a million pieces she didn't want to deal with this on her own, but she had no choice, if she were to have future hopefully with the man that just walked out the door, if only she could get him to see past the lies and her past.

CHAPTER 31

"Sabrina, are you there bitch!?" Jared angerly shout at his exes wishing he could have seen the look on Sabrina face when her lover boy walked out on her like her dad did when she told him her sob story of her dad abandoning when she was young he did feel sorry for her for a second, but chuckled to her as he mocked her "ahh did Loverboy see you for the lying slut that you are and walked out". Heat ran and coldness ran through Sabrina's vanes she needed to think of a plan to get Julia and everyone that might be harmed, she didn't care what happened to her. Ranning out of patience with Jared and his mocking Sabrina shout at him "What the hell do you want, please let Julia go she has nothing to do with this period, if you want me why don't you come after me instead?" she pleaded with him, trying to reach the man that she thought she loved a long time ago before she knew what he was really like "look bitch you know what I want and this trying to get to my soft side isn't going to work, I don't have a soft spot you killed that a long time ago, but I do love to hear you begging for the life of someone else, maybe I should sweet the deal even further with you and lure you lover boy making sure I get what I want, but instead I have this lovely creature Brenda that has a thing for your lover too why I don't know, right babe, speak as Brenda's sobbing voice comes over the phone pleading with Sabrina to help her as well even though Sabrina didn't care for Brenda, she didn't want to see anyone get hurt from Jared. "Fine, what do you want" Sabrina demanded. Jared told her exactly what he wanted her to bring all the evidence that she had against him, he gave her the directions, but she told him that she didn't have car to get where he wanted to her to be at, Jared didn't care if she wanted to see these ladies a live she would do anything she can to save them this wasn't about her this was about saving Julia and Brenda's lives, were at stack Jared was giving her one hour to get to where he was he forced her to write down the direction. Jared smiled to himself after he hung up the phone loving that his plan is coming together as he recalls the look of pure terror spreading across Sabrina face when she saw him through the large glass window of the Diner it was priceless to him, he wanted to know the outcome from Brenda, but he didn't expect the old hag of Jack's mother following Brenda to the hotel, where Jared was staying at he wanted to get out of this dry up Texas land with less people knowing about him as little as possible he guessed he had to get more bullets he couldn't leave any witnesses alive, so be it. Jared smirked to himself.

Jack listens intently at the door that he left slightly opened pretending to walk out, because he felt in his gut there was more going on with this phone call because she sounded upset on the phone then ice course through his vanes when he heard his mother's name being mentioned he wanted to demand what was going on, but he feared that he would get more lies then the truth, so he remained quiet where he was, he could since something wasn't right if his mother was involve and he could tell that this phone call right way had nothing to do with her father that it was Jared her ex that she was talking to and she was not happy talking him. Then a clap of thunder could be heard over head letting everyone around them the storm was approaching, in more ways than one Jack thought has he heard the phone ending, with what Jack could hear from inside of the apartment that Sabrina was rushed toward her bed room.

Sabrina rushed towards her bedroom when she notice that her door was slightly open, which confused her, she thought she saw Jack closed the door when he left. She looks outside seeing no one there, she goes back to what she needed to do get the suitcase that had all of Jared paper work and plus the gun that she had stashed there that one of her good friends that she knew from high school, dad who was cop taught her how to shot and to defend herself that she needed to do right now if she played her cards right now. Sabrina thumbs through the yellow pages for a cab that could drive her where she needed to go in a hurry like right now looks at her watch, she only had 45 minutes to get to where Jared was at. She looked at the directions that she was given, and she froze, of all the places in the world he had to pick was a cabin in the woods. Sabrina wasn't hoping it wasn't Jack's cabin, she didn't want what Jared has in store for her mar the beautiful memory she shared with Jack, with their love making, the tenderness and the pure trust Jack had her to vanished into thin air, but she guessed that already did.

CHAPTER 32

"This is Trapper Jon disembodied voice comes over the air "hoping you all are staying trapped inside your house folks, because the storm is coming, the authorities are telling everyone to stay off the streets unless you have to" the deejay complained on the air about being there instead of being in his home, but his fans lives where more important than his whined a little he joked a little to lighten the mood. Sabrina wished her mood could be lightened a little too, but she couldn't she needed to get to where Jared was fast and figure out a way to outsmart Jared that they all could survive all this, she hoped as she nervously wait in the cab as it speed onto and up the windy road that lead up to the mountains "God no!"she thought has the cab comes closer to the cabin that was Jack's cabin her worst fears were coming true as the cab parks in front of the cabin. The cabbie wanted to stay, but Sabrina reassured the cabbie that she would be ok, she felt like she was being watched she didn't see anyone, she then watched the cabbie pull a way wishing it was taking her away, she just needed to push through this.

"Well, well, isn't it my long-lost slut, of an ex" Jared appears at the top of the stairs in a dark figure when a clashed of lightening came through lighting everything around them for a second. "What do you think?" Jared boasted with his arms out stretched " I thought I would make you feel at home when you breath your last?" Jared mocked "where is Julia and Brenda?" Sabrina demanded ignoring his mocked statement, she knows that this was the last place that she wanted to be at remembering the last time she was in Jared presence with her running for her life in a forest much like this one, but the last time she was in a cabin was with Jack, she didn't want the last image of her surviving mar this place forever this was Jack's place. She didn't want Jared to know that, with him still bring up bad memories that she wants to forget.

Jack watched in horror the woman that he loved was standing at the foot of the steps that was his place and not the man that was leaning down saying what Jack couldn't hear what was being said, but it wasn't good from the man. Jack was assuming was Jared was flinging his arms about and Sabrina was not happy to see him, Jack could tell.

"Jared! Where are they!?" Sabrina snapped getting pist by the second with Jared's mind game with him stalling, she wanted to get this over with "what no hi and how are you doing after you're the one left me to care for myself you know, I nearly died or do you even care, to bad your lover boy isn't here because I would love for him to see how careless you are with nearly killing me with that poker and stealing from me." Jared snared at his ex "after what you did to all those innscent people that trusted you with their hard earn savings, then you used me as well when you suppose to love me or was that a lie too. I was defending myself against you. I was 19 years old a young girl who trusted you, but then you used me, could use what you did against me, but in my stupidty I believed in you, I don't want to talk about that, where are Julia and Brenda?" Sabrina asked again trying to get things back on track "I don't know are they here?" Jared mocked again shrugging his shoulders pointing a knife at her that she can see that there was a little blood on it, was it Julia's or Brenda she didn't know she wanted them to be safe and away from this crazy man, she thought.

Jack's caught his breath in his lunges when he heard his mom's name being mentioned, maybe he should have warned the cabbie he saw pulled away to get help, but right now he needed to figure out what was going on, why his mother was involved in this and get everyone out of this alive, right now he needed to wait and see what Jared or Sabrina does to change things this wait and see game that they were playing which wasn't setting well with him, waiting on someone else to make the next move that he should make.

"Well, my dear until I get what I wanted" Jared glared at Sabrina loving the power that he was waving about like a sword like he was the hero and not the villain in this piece, Jared thought proudly wow he was winning this round. He need to continue to win because he didn't like losing when so much was at steak the sooner he gets this over with the better for him, when he has miles between him and this town, Jared thought keeping his focus on the woman before him, keep stalling and play his mind game as the rain began to come down hard on them both, loving the fact this was a nightmare for Sabrina even thou she is acting more tough then she was before, like the rain and the sight of the cabin did not fazed her anymore Jared didn't like this sight of his ex all brave and shit, he wanted her to fear him as she begged him to spare her life as it slipped through his fingers. "Jared, I want to see Julia and Brenda first that I know they are save before I give you want you want!" Sabrina demanded raising her head showing him that she didn't feared him, which she didn't has she climbed the steps one at a time coming toward Jared showing him that she wasn't scared of him any more thanks to Jack, which was pisting him off more he wanted her to coward before him which would give him more power over her. He grabs her by the right arm showing her that he meant business, but she still didn't show any fear towards him like she didn't care about her own life just those stupid bitches that were being helded at the hotel that he left tied up. Jared threw her into the cabin wanting to get this thing started and over with and be on his way.

Sabrina looks around her remembering her time with Jack how he would make love up stairs and, on the couch, as her inside tighten as if her body was recalling her wonderful time here that is one memory that if she dies here tonight will take with her.

Then she sees Jared stalked towards her causing to back up getting herself ready for whatever he had in stored for her, that is when she sees Jared reaches back to backhands her right across her right cheek causing to her reach for her cheek with her hand, she felt fire on her cheek causing her stumble little and felt the metal taste on her tongue from the blood that enter her mouth, and then Jared continued the attack on Sabrina causing to fall to the floor, crawling toward the fireplace looking for anything that she could use has a weapon against Jared when she remembered the gun that she had at her waist band of her pants, she was wearing still in her uniform., but she couldn't get to it without him knowing that she had it with her.

Jack watched in horror the woman he loved getting beaten through window of the door to see what was happening he wanted to get in there to save Sabrina then he sees a thick branch that could do some major damage.

Jared continue his attack on Sabrina laughing and smiling when he felt he was winning the round when he heard a crash behind him, being atackled from a mad truck as the wind was being almost knocked out of him. Then he turned to see whom his attacker was he was in shocked that Sabrina lover boy has come to her rescue this time which pisted him off big time he wanted to be the winner in this and now this Jack person has come to be the hero in this Jared didn't like this one bit, he found the knife that he found in the kitchen turn on his attacker getting ready to stab him when he felt a sharp kick to his gut doubling over in pain, then he felt a knee to Jared's face than he felt his nose break and he tasted his blood in his mouth making it hard to breathe a little, but he was still determined to win this one at all cost. Then Jared pushed into Jack causing him to fall back on his back. Jack was in shock how tough this jack ass was that he was used to fighting and he was strong. Jack will fight with all his might to make sure everyone gets out alive.

CHAPTER 33

Sabrina was still lying on the hard wood that was covered with area rug with every part of her body hurting, but she was alive, then she heard angry voices coming from the same room she was in that were muffed little and flesh being hit as wells, but it wasn't hers this time. Sabrina thought she was hearing another voice other than Jared's cursing her this time. Maybe she was imaging things, she was hearing Jack's voice, she was having a hard time getting her body to move like she want it hurt like hell. Sabrina slowly moves up on her arms to see where the fight was coming from to her horror was Jack was on his knees struggling to gain control over the situation, but it looking like it Jared that was having the upper hand with Jack with his right arm wrapped around his large shoulder's getting ready to slice Jack's neck with a large butcher large getting ready to use it on Jack's neck to slice from ear to ear. Sabrina struggled up a lttle she felt she was 100 miles away from her man. She could not let the man of her dreams die before and let Jared win this round anymore she needed to end it no matter what the out come might be. Jack was to good for that she just needed to save him and then figure out where to go from here. Sabrina remembered her gun that she was laying underneath that must have fallen from her waist that was hidden when she arrived to the cabin moments ages ago, a gift from a friend.

Sabrina steadies herself even thou every inch of her body was screaming in pain, but she must mustard through the pain to save Jack he needed her and she needed him.

Jack could believe how strong this mother fucker was and how he was allowing this asshole to get the upper hand he didn't know, but he needed to fight through this save the woman he loved more then anything.

Then Sabrina voice shouted toward Jared to get his attention away from Jack back to her "JARED! Let him go!" she demanded; Jared glared at the bitch that was still laying on the floor "BITCH! why don't you just die already!" Jared mocked, than he saw the barrel of the gun aimed at him in shock he didn't even notice that she was carrying, he didn't think she was that smart, but here she was a gun in both hands taking control of the situation, making sure that they both get out of this one piece especially Jack, that she didn't want him cought up in this situation this was supposed to between Jared and her. "Go to HELL!" then she pulled the trigger and heard the gun exploded then the bullet firing straight toward Jared freezed in shock and then crumbled to the floor like he was ragged doll as the blood from the bullet wound starting oozing with his blood down his face where Sabrina shoot him in the forehead right between the eyes. Sabrina felt the room began to spin and fade into black as she closed her eyes, then she felt arms cradle her into strong arms trying to wake her up, trying to keep her a live so the ambulance could there it was a long drive where they are right now. Jack was doing anything to keep her awake so he could take her to hospital. "Darling, stay with me okay," Jack pegging her to stay with him. "Where is your mother, Jared had your mother and Brenda that is why he told me to come, I am sorry. Your need to go and find her, please Jack leave me here go find." Sabrina barely whispered to him trying hard to convence him to leave her to go and find his mother she didn't want him to see her like she was better off without him, "Sabrina, Honey I am going where you are , you need to hang in there the ambulance is on the way, you just need to hang on there, don't leve me." Jack begged the woman that come to be more to him then another woman another than his mother. Jack was looking over her injuried body trying to figure out what he could do to help save or keep her alive, a long enough so he could get her help. Then with horror she fell silenct again then Jack began to shack her, even pounding on her chest to her to wake up, but there was so much blood that he didn't how to stop the blood, but he could hear the sirens screaming off indistance he was begging to them to hurry up, he did want to lose her as he begged to stay with the help was almost here. "Jack, I am sorry for lying to you, I I I want you to know, I love you" Sabrina whispered she wanted her last words to Jack mean something him even if she did lied him that he meant the world to her even if their time together was short, but sweet to her as her vision began to blare to fade to black and she could hear Jack voice off into the distance shouting her to stay with him, don't leave and trying hard to stay awake, the pain and lose of blood was to much for her tiny body to take.

"SABRINA……!!!!"

Sabrina slowly opens her eyes trying hard to adjust her eyesight toward the brightness of the daylight she didn't know where she was then the pain of her body brought her awareness that she was in a hospital, she was trying hard to remember how she got her, she then hears the beeps of the heart monitor near her and the switshed of the oxygen machine breathing for her. Sabrina tried to move up to adjust comfortable in the bed that she was in, but the pain was much for her, the pain took her breath away. Then she realizes she was alone in the room that was no sign of anyone not even Jack, she wondered where he was, she was getting scared that something happened to him that maybe Jared did something to him, but then she remembered that she had killed him in the fight up in the cabin.

"Hey beautiful, you are awake!" Jack said softly, trying hard to be strong for her he was so scared that she won't wake up soon, but he was told she was a fighter and he choice to believe that she was a fighter she was the strongest woman he had ever met besides his mother and that she won't give up not just like that. She had been through so much, but he didn't want to add to her pain, Jack did some soul searching with all that happened with the short amount time they had and how quickly they (Sabrina and him) got so hot and heavy. They really don't know each very well and Jack couldn't get the idea out of his head that she lied to him about her past and she put his mother's life endanger even she wasn't responsible for Jared, but if she told the truth maybe this nightmare would not have happened.

Sabrina looks at Jack he was so handsome with his exotic, lean muscular, he was so tall and his hair that was like the fall of night, dark eyes that pulled her in whenever he looked at her, but she could tell that something was off with him maybe something happened with his mom. "Jack, are you ok, did something happen to your mom, please tell me thar she is okay." She demands getting scared with his silence "no, she is fine, the cops found her at the motel that Jared was staying at, she was a little shaking up, but she is fine." He answered glad to see the relief come over the beautiful face of Sabrina. "We do need to talk thou, about us though" Jack said trying hard not to lose it in front her because he didn't want to break her heart because he needed to put some distance between her and him, he knew that this was shitty thing to do because she needed to focus on healing he just hope that this doesn't put that healing on hold, but he didn't do this there will be no chance for them both if there was an us. Sabrina didn't like the distance she felt from Jack, like he was preparing her for something unpleasant and she was right. "Look, I know timing of this isn't good, but I need to put some distance between you and I because we got so hot and heavy so quickly that we barely knew each other and right now I have to focus on my music that I have lost track on and I have a world tour coming, I am not going to have time for a relationship right now and you need to focus on healing right now and I will be here for you, to help you get on your feet. "Jack said sheepishly he didn't like the look of hurt in her eyes like he just slapped her in the face, then she pulled away from him, he wanted to keep on holding her, he wanted her to see that was for the best, but now he wasn't sure. Sabrina felt heart dropped and snapped into two in her chest that if she moved it would break into a million ore pieces, but she didn't want Jack to see that so she asked in a brave voice "are you breaking up with me?" she asked trying hard to keep her tears at bay so he doesn't see them those where for her and not for him, her yet again another man that was supposed to be important to her turn their backs on her and walking away. "No, this isn't a breakup this putting distance between us" Jack trying hard convinced her that he wasn't ending their relationship, he just needed some space.

Just then the doctor knocks on the door causing

them to stop their talk at the moment "Hi I am Doctor Maxwell, I am your doctor just want to check on you to see if your awake and see how you are doing, I hope this isn't a bad timing?" the doctor asked. Sabrina pops in "no you timing is perfect doctor." To cheerfully wanting to change the subject to keep her heart from breaking more and show Jack that she didn't need him anyways, she will be fine without him anyways. "I just need to check your vitals and see how you are heeling I will be quick; I promise!" Doctor said, "you can stay, Mr. Taylor, I will be brief!" "No! he was just leaving." Sabrina snapped wanting him to leave as quickly as possible so she could be alone again and move on from him. "You're sure I will be just outside, and I need to make some calls too." Jack feeling like a complete ass right now because the last thing he wanted to do was crush this amazing woman's heart, but he needed to do something to make things right with her and make her see that he wasn't ending things with her.

Moments later after the doctor left, Sabrina sat on her bed she asked the doctor when would she be ok to go back to work, in a few weeks when he told her and that she needed to get some rest and take it slowly the next few weeks. Sabrina didn't care at the moment she never felt so alone and scared in her life right now, she didn't have to worry about Jared anymore she was freed from her past, but her future was now in questioned, 'Thank you God, she looked up to the ceiling giving thanks to her maker, she was sure the cops would want to talk to her about what happened, right now she wanted to cry then the tears start to flow down her cheeks she wanted the ground to open up and swallow her. Then she felt the warm hand on her left shoulder that caused her to stop her crying and then she looked up to see Jack there "why are you crying?" he asked softly he gently got into bed with her to comfort her as she continued her crying*****

The end for now!?